PRESENTE

A Dockworker Story

By Herb Mills

Library of Congress Cataloging-in-Publication Data:

Mills, Herb

Presente, A Dockworker Story

1. International Longshore and Warehouse Union 2. San Francisco 3. Dockworker 4. El Salvador military regime 5. Social justice 6. Labor Union 7. Labor and social justice. Herb Mills.

While this novel is a work of fiction, it is inspired by actual historical events. Some characters are fictional; names and titles are created for dramatic effect. Events have been depicted according to historical union documents and the author's recollections.

Editing by Peter Cole, Stephanie Fay, Matthew Tallon.

Cover art work and map of the Embardcadero by Marc Nelson, of marcnelsonart.com.

Book formatting for digital printing by Matthew Tallon, Dublin, Ireland.

Published by Hard Ball Press, Brooklyn, New York.

Information at: www.hardballpress.com

ISBN: 979-8-9850979-9-3

*To the founders, members, and pensioners of the
ILWU, Solidarity!*

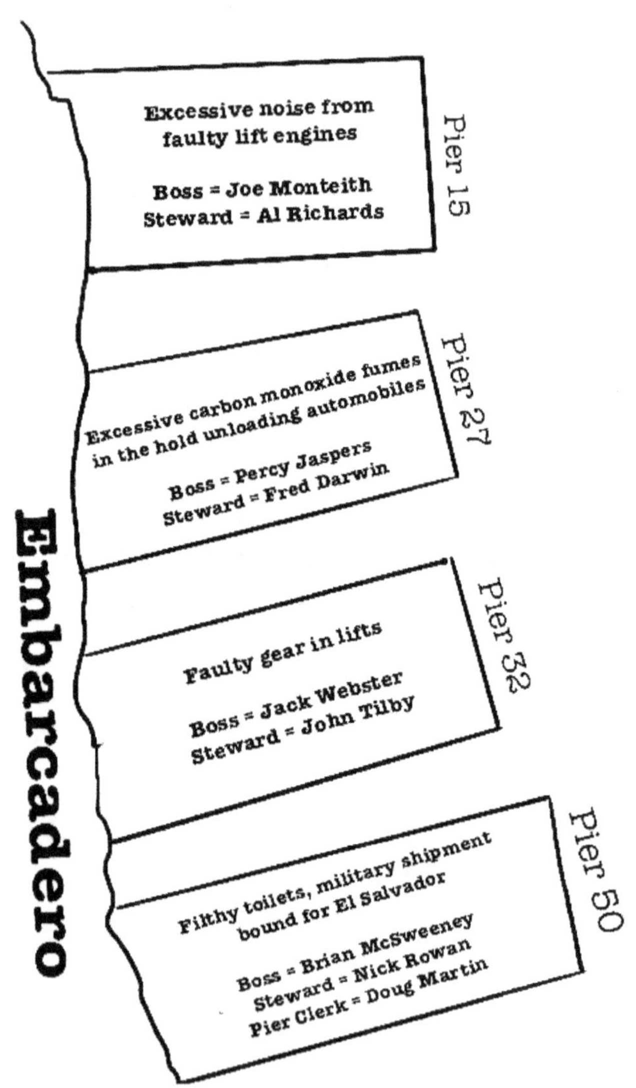

San Francisco
Embarcadero
Excessive noise from
faulty lift engines

Boss = Joe Monteith
Steward = Al Richards
Pier 15
Excessive carbon monoxide fumes
in the hold unloading automobiles

Boss = Percy Jaspers
Steward = Fred Darwin
Pier 27
Faulty gear in lifts

Boss = Jack Webster
Steward = John Tilby
Pier 32
Filthy toilets, military shipment
bound for El Salvador

Boss = Brian McSweeney
Steward = Nick Rowan
Pier Clerk = Doug Martin
Pier 50

GLOSSARY OF NAMES & ORGANIZATIONS

Al Richards: ILWU steward at Pier 15, argued with Boss Joe Montieth over excessive noise from lifts.

Bill Hanson: ILWU International Vice President.

Clerk on the Docks: the dock clerk is responsible for overseeing and managing the daily operations of docks or piers at shipping yards, ports or logistics facilities. They track all the goods loading and unloading to the ships.

Doug Martin: A clerk and union member at Pier 50 who feeds Steve crucial information about the arms shipment bound for El Salvador.

Father Robert McGinnis: head of the San Francisco Archdiocesan staff and chair of its Social Justice Commission.

FDR: The Frente Democrático Revolucionario (Democratic Revolutionary Front) – an anti-fascist group in El Salvador.

Frank Spaulding: ILWU member in Local 10 who edits the Local 10 union newsletter.

FUPS: United Salvadoran Patriotic Forces, a violent, pro-junta front group active in the US.

Guillermo Hernandez: a junta leader orchestrating violence in the US.

Gus Vincenti: An honest union leader at a West Coast Local fighting against mob incursion.

Harvey Garrison: An ILWU traveling steward.

ILWU: The International Longshore and Warehouse Union (originally, The International Longshoremen's and Warehousemen's

Union) represents dockworkers and warehouse workers in the US and Canada.

Jack Mahoney: President of ILWU Local 19 in Seattle.

Jim Birch: A sympathetic news reporter for the *San Francisco Chronicle*.

Joe Margolis: International Vice President, ILWU.

John Boyer: A minister with the San Francisco Archdiocese Social Justice Commission and staff of the World Council of Churches.

John Tilby: A union steward at Pier 32 who complained about faulty winches that boss Webster demanded they use to load the Tropic Tide.

LRC: The Labor Relations Committee: a forum where the PCMA and the

union meet to hash out issues.

Margarito Montebon: An honest union leader at a West Coast Local fighting against mob incursion.

Maria Martinez: An activist for El Salvador human rights.

Michael McSweeney: An unreasonable terminal boss on Pier 50.

Nick Rowan: An ILWU steward for Pier 50 who first notifies Steve Morrow of the arms shipment earmarked for El Salvador.

Norman Rowe: A CBS television producer.

Paul Murphy: International President, ILWU based in San Francisco.

PCMA: The Pacific Coast Marine Association, represents the steamship companies doing business with and hiring the dockworkers.

Reynolds: A VP for the Tropic Steamship Company.

Russ Taylor: A retired ILWU member who tackles asbestos payment from company

Sister Mary Margaret: A member of the San Francisco Archdiocese staff.

Sister Catherine Anne: A Maryknoll Nun recently returned from El Salvador.

Spencer: A CBS producer for 60 Minutes TV show.

Steve Morrow: Officer for ILWU Local 10.

Susan Vogel: A photojournalist hired by the AFL-CIO to cover union issues.

Tom Augustine : A leader of the Social Justice Commission for the San Francisco Archdiocese.

Tony Tristelli: A mob boss taking over a West Coast Local.

Pete Turner: International Secretary Treasurer, ILWU

Thornton: A representative and stooge for Tropic Steamship Company.

Webster: An unreasonable superintendent on the dock.

Wednesday, December 3, 1980

I rolled into the dock parking lot at my usual time–ten to six–hoping for a quiet day. I had met up with an old pal visiting Frisco the night before and was still feeling the effects. It was strange for me to be hung over. Come a morning I always hit the road feeling sharp, but today I barely managed to make it out of the house with the decks awash.

Getting out of my trusty old '73 Dodge, I was immediately met by half a dozen guys who stuck around after the night shift waiting to catch me as soon as I got in. I knew right away I wasn't going to get my quiet day. Still, I had no idea just how unquiet things were about to become.

Although everybody talked at once, I caught the gist of the problem as we moved through the slackening rain toward my office. They had been asked to lash some cargo on a shipment fresh in from Hong Kong aboard the *Astral Tide*, and conditions just weren't safe. Railings less than 30 inches high on narrow platforms and a twelve-foot clearing. Any worker fell, he'd be straight in the drink.

They had tried to explain the situation to the terminal boss, a guy with a sour puss and even more sour breath named Michael McSweeney, but he just started the usual jive. So they put down their tools. Now they wanted to make sure the dayside gang would also refuse to do the unsafe work.

We had some good fun scheming what to do next. As a

union officer for the San Francisco Bay Local 10 of the ILWU (The International Longshoremen's and Warehousemen's Union), my most and least favorite part of the job were the same thing—wrestling with the folks on the other side; the bosses who didn't give a goddamn about us dockworkers or our safety. I felt incredible whenever I got a victory for the workers, but the endless fight was wearing. Depressing, even.

We decided if boss McSweeney failed to come up with a safe method to unload the boxes, they'd call Local 10 to try and reach me. But when they did that, they'd "discover" I was tied up seeing a lawyer on behalf of an injured worker. That'd buy them a couple of hours. Then, once McSweeney *did* reach me, I'd school him on every damn thing that was wrong with that work site. We all felt pretty snappy with our plan.

The day continued with a run of routine matters. A couple of guys complaining about fines for missing a membership meeting. A brother asking about his dues while he was off hurt. An old pensioner, wanting to know what Labor would do now that Reagan had been elected.

I snorted, "That's a damn good question."

Another guy came into my office to request clearance to travel. A lot of the dockers go working in other West Coast ports to clear their heads. As I signed the guy's release papers, I found myself getting jealous of his travel plans. I was ready to go, too. Two terms as a union officer fighting the bosses on the waterfront had worn me out.

When I heard the intercom buzzing for what felt like the 80th time that day, I suspected it was McSweeney wanting to jive me about his lousy boxes just before the shift begins. My response ready to go, I answered.

"Yeah?"

"Steve, Nick Rowan's calling for you from Pier Fifty-B."

"Five minutes to start-up time. He's on his schedule."

Nick phoned so often he never turned up to work without a pocketful of dimes for the payphone. Still, Nick was okay. Too many calls to the union from a steward was better than no calls. I hit the transfer button.

"Hey, old bud, what's doing?"

"Listen, Steve. I'm here at Fifty-B, okay?"

I could hear the tension in Nick's voice. This was no petty gripe.

"Yeah?"

"What would you say to a shipment of weapons to El Salvador?"

Yep. Another quiet day on the docks.

A year ago in October, 1979, my union supported the bloodless coup that sought to install civilian rule in El Salvador, *and* opposed any counterrevolution from the dictatorial and repressive military junta. We had also supported Monsignor Oscar Romero, the nation's courageous archbishop, when he sent a wire to then-President Jimmy Carter warning him that any military aid would only worsen the junta's oppression of a people who were seeking their basic rights.

Shortly after sending that wire, the archbishop was killed in a hail of gunfire by one of the government's many death squads, and the "reformist" government soon launched a long, bloody civil war, committing horrible atrocities against the people, including women and children. In the wake of these developments, Ronald Reagan's presidential campaign was sounding the drums of war. Soon after, the union decided that if and when we learned of any further military aid being sent from any ports we worked, we would immediately announce our refusal to load it.

We developed a plan that included soliciting public support for our action. But we had no illusions. Even if we held out for a long time, the junta could arrange to ship the arms by another route, just as Romero had feared. But we hoped we could slow down the delivery, or at least foster a public discussion about justice.

Memories of that past year's struggle rose up and smacked me on the head as I sat there holding the phone. Gathering my thoughts, I asked Nick what was in the shipment.

"There are lots of crates marked 'gas grenades,' 'protective masks,' 'body armor'." I frantically scribbled down everything on Nick's list. "Then they've got radio sets and all the stuff to go with them. Also, there are crates of medical stuff and something marked 'Field Hospital,' but more than half of it all is stenciled with the words 'Safety and Rescue Equipment'."

We both knew we had to find out what that equipment was. And soon.

"Where is this stuff?"

"Down in Shed D. Which these days is basically a parking lot for City Maintenance Vehicles. Might be it's down there to keep it hidden. I only saw it 'cause I was in the Shed trying to do a halfway decent job cleaning the crapper. The *Tropic Moon* had five gangs, and there's been no cleaning at all of the toilet. It's a sight to behold, Steve. Really disgusting. I was actually going to call you about it when I discovered the gear for El Salvador."

Perfect. The lousy crapper would give me the excuse I needed to get down there and check out this 'aid'.

"Look, Nick. What ship is this cargo supposed to be loaded aboard?"

"It's all for the *Tropic Moon,* but she just sailed for Seattle."

"Great. She should be laid up there for a couple of weeks. That buys us a little time. Nick, I'm gonna come out there right now. Make a point of telling the guys I'm coming to look at the crapper."

"You got it."

Hanging up, I suddenly didn't feel lousy and worn out anymore. Anxious, sure. But riled up all the same, a fire in my belly.

I pulled out my address book and dialed Tom Augustine, the head of the Social Justice Commission for the San Francisco Archdiocese. I knew he led a monthly meeting of religious folks concerned about the people of Central America. Tom was always involved in a lot of things–stretched thin by the ongoing sins of this weary old world and by our politically active staff. Still, like always he greeted me with a bouncy, "Morning, Steve! How are things on the waterfront?"

I used the code we had agreed upon: "How about a shipment south?"

This was met with stunned silence. I heard the rain on my windowpane and the mist-muffled moan of a distant foghorn.

"Oh my God," he finally replied. "When can we meet?"

"I'm heading over there to take a look and get some photos. Barring the unforeseen, I could be at your place at eleven."

"Well, would you believe that our monthly group will be here at nine to discuss what we should try to do now that Reagan's been elected? Your news may save us some time."

Tom offered to call a friend in Washington who works for the Conference of Catholic Bishops. We planned out some next steps, then said our goodbyes.

Hustling out of the office to my old Dodge with its 100k hard miles on the odometer, I grinned with pride when the engine turned over on the first try.

3

Although the rain had stopped, a lingering mist muted the noise around the wharf and softened the lights as I headed down North Point toward the waterfront. For those of us who work on that line of the docks, the once bustling Embarcadero is now a land of ghosts. Of things no longer there. When we drive or walk along it, we experience flashbacks to its former color and bustle; the scenes and encounters with the folks who fashioned our heritage but are no longer with us. Memories of the union and the waterfront I knew as a kid.

My dad hitched to Frisco from Detroit when he was twenty-two. That was in 1932. He landed a job at a warehouse in the Mission District and later became a proud charter member of ILWU Local 6, which still represents warehouse workers in the Bay Area.

I was born in 1941. When I was a kid my dad took me with him to the big, coast-wide dockworker strikes in '46 and '48. Sometimes he took me to see the dockers working the ships that crowded the finger piers all along the Embarcadero. He was so proud when, after finishing high school, I, too, joined the ILWU as a longshoreman in Local 10.

I put aside the past as I pulled into Pier 50, focusing on the task at hand. The towering steel hulk of a cargo ship loomed over me, its proud bow jutting out high over the water. I stopped at a low shack at the end of Shed B where the clerks for the incoming and outgoing ships work and went in to call my answering service. Doug Martin, a stocky fellow with a handlebar mustache, is the dock clerk for the *Tropic Moon*. He's responsible for overseeing and managing the daily operations at the port, including tracking all of the goods loaded or unloaded on the ships.

Soon as I stepped into his office, Doug sang out, "Steve! What's cooking, buddy?"

I told him how our steward Nick Rowan discovered the government plan to load the military weapons on Pier 50 for the junta in El Salvador.

"Jesus." Doug's handlebar mustache drooped as he took in the bad news. He immediately grabbed a folder marked *Tropic Moon.*

"I'll be damned," he tutted, leafing through the files. "We gotta say no to this. Can we legally refuse to load this gear?"

"That's just what I'm going to check out."

"So, you'll be needing copies?" He held up the files, a twinkle in his baby blues.

"Doug, my boy, you read my mind."

He said he'd run off the copies right away, since the terminal boss McSweeney wasn't in yet (no surprise).

I told him about Nick and the crappy crapper and we refined a plan. I'd go see terminal boss McSweeney, tying him up at his desk with a lecture on public health while Doug made copies of the file. But first I needed to get some snaps of the cargo. If I was spotted down there, I'd say I'd gone down there to take a look at the shitty shitter.

I got to admit, I was enjoying myself. The excitement of putting one over on the bosses–well, that's the best cure for a hangover there is.

4

In quick order I carried out the inspection of the problem toilets and saw good cause for complaint. Then I went over to Shed D. Standing in the loading bay, I looked up and down the pier. No sign of boss McSweeney…or anybody else. The fog was drifting in off the water, just like in the movies, as I slipped quickly into the shed and stood still for a moment in the shadows.

Not a sound.

I got my snaps of the "aid" shipment, then I exited the shed, keeping to the shadows, and made my way down to the bunker of one Mister Michael McSweeney.

McSweeney was in his regular working posture reading the sports section with his feet up on the desk. He had a large, knobby head, a thick mat of reddish-blond hair and a big, close-shaved mug set between monstrous ears and dark, shifty eyes.

Spotting me, he made a point of folding his paper as slowly as possible, then said: "You know, the fact is, you've got yourself a damn good job."

I grinned at him and took the better of the two easy chairs in front of his desk.

"And you've got a great sense of humor."

He lit up a Camel and blew some smoke my way.

"So what's the fucking beef today?"

"The crapper in Shed D. I got a call about it and had a peek. In case you don't know, it's a threat to public health."

McSweeney sighed and shook his head. I knew he was thinking what a pain in the ass I was. Still, he had to speak carefully.

"So, what's the problem, at least to you?"

"Well, four stools are plugged and full, so it's nasty. Even if the stools may still be flushing, there is water all over the floor. The drains don't work, and the troughs all stink. There is no paper in most of the stalls. And besides, there's no soap."

"Jesus Christ! Look, you fucking well know we had five gangs on the *Moon* instead of four. What do you want from me, scented candles and hot towels?"

"Well, the question really is, what do *you* want? Say, for example, a couple hours to get things right? Or something a little more…long-term?"

He waved his hands and shuffled a bunch of papers around his desk, trying to look in charge even though he knew he'd lost.

"Okay. A *couple* of hours."

"For starters."

He got up to leave the office. Crap. I didn't realize he'd roll over that quick. Doug needed more time to copy that file.

"Hey wait a sec! I'm not done. The fact is, none of your crappers comply with the new OSHA rules."

The pier boss pinched the bridge of his nose. "Your saying that doesn't make it so. I don't know of a rule we're not following, for crappers or anything else."

"Well, let me fill you in on the fine points of the new crapper code."

"Oh, I would *love* to hear them."

"Well, there's a new rule on stalls for one thing. I don't know if you've noticed this from your desk, but women work here, too. Not everybody can just piss in a trough. We need stalls." Of course, I was the one who was stalling.

"Jesus Christ."

"And speaking of troughs," I went on, "new rules say they have to be done according to a formula. So many feet of trough per male worker. And they have to be a particular depth and width.

The blank look on his face made me want to laugh. I tried to keep my tone as severe as possible.

"It may sound funny to you, and maybe it is funny, but what we've got here is a science on shitters."

McSweeney narrowed his eyes and shot back: "What the fuck is this, anyway!"

Afraid he might have caught on I was screwing with him, I tried to act insulted: "Hey now, wait a minute! It may sound goofy, but we've both got our duties here. And the men have their duties. And they need proper restroom facilities in order to properly perform *their* duties."

"Okay! I'll look into this 'science' of yours. But if you got a beef, really, it's with the port, we're just the tenant."

I knew he was going to try and pass the buck like that. He went on. "The port's the one who built these piers. So if the crappers are no good, who's really to blame? I mean, I don't got no magic wand here."

"Yeah, well maybe you better find the good fairy who can supply one, 'cause when the shit hits the fan–which it will soon if these men have nowhere else to relieve themselves– the question won't be who's to blame. It's who's gonna *pay*. And that's gonna be you."

"How do you figure?"

I smirked. "Let me tell you a story."

"Jesus Christ! Not more of your waterfront lore, Steve, I've got no time for it."

I knew how much the guy loved my old dock stories.

"Once upon a time-I mean, it was only a couple of months ago–the crappers over at Pier 40 were something like yours. Drains plugged, faucets broken, and some of the seats were gone, so they could pinch a customer."

"Or de-ball one." He smirked at his own joke, so I figured I'd make him frown.

"Anyway, the pier boss said he was just the tenant. So guess what we did? The next meeting we had, the health department came along to join us. By the end of that meeting they ordered that each can be closed in turn until it was fully up to code, steam cleaned and painted, *and* a trailer-mounted washroom and a dozen porta potties were to be rented and placed nearby while the crappers were under repair."

As the light drained from McSweeney's face, I brought it all home. "You know what else?"

"What?"

"He said that to avoid any waiting in line, anyone 'in need' could leave the job to find a can uptown. As a result, four ships got delayed by something over four hours. And with all those folks heading for town, the morning and afternoon coffee time was something else."

The boss sighed, weary and defeated. "I get the drift."

Figuring Doug had surely finished up by now, I stood up, a victorious smile on my face.

"Well, a damn good rap. Don't take any wooden nickels, watch the game, and I'll be back on Tuesday."

On my way out of the dock, I saw Doug approaching with a large envelope in his hand. He assured me it had been "no problem at all." We both laughed about our cake walk and I promised I'd be in touch, then pulled away. I couldn't stop smiling the whole drive to see Tom Augustine at the Archdiocese.

5

On my way to the Archdiocese I stopped at a camera shop over on Ellis and Polk to get my snaps developed. I dropped off the film, then went to the coffee shop next door to review Doug's paperwork. There were four folders, labelled: "Hardware," "Medical," "Radio Equipment," and "Safety and Rescue Equipment." I noticed that while the first three folders had items listed by name–"Gas Grenades," "Gauze," "Radio Set with accessories and cables," etcetera–the Safety and Rescue Equipment was only listed by an "S&R" number. Why did none of it get listed by name?

I took out a new folder, labeled it "Junta Military Aid, December 3, 1980," and wrote down everything I knew. Picking at my bear claw on my table, I got to pondering how the union, once we refused on-site to load the cargo, could be forced to change its mind. Such a refusal violated the union's contract with the Pacific Coast Marine Association (PCMA), which had among its membership 125 steamship lines, stevedore firms, and terminals up and down the Pacific Coast.

The PCMA would quickly move to arbitration. If the union stood firm in its refusal, they could take us to court and win easily. The contract was clear: we didn't get to decide which cargo to load or unload, so we'd be subject to a fine.

If we continued to refuse, the court would levy a large daily fine until we loaded the military supplies. Under the heading "Contract & Legal" I jotted down all this info, then added up the potential cost of all this. Half the arbitration costs, attorneys' fees, increasingly higher fines, very high damages, and the jailing of some union officers. When you totaled it all up it looked more like a Social Security Number than an acceptable expense.

Having listed all these drawbacks, I went on to note the way the union could prevail. The PCMA would have to represent the parties damaged by the refusal: the owner of the *Moon*, the stevedore firm that had the contract to work the ship when it was berthed at Pier 50-B, and the government, as shipper. If the government canceled the shipment, however, neither the ship nor the stevedores would have a legitimate legal complaint.

The bottom line was that the government just *might* cancel the aid if we gained enough support from the public. That's how we'd done it back in '78. However, given Reagan's victory and the political landscape today, the way we gained support would have to be different, and the support would have to be even stronger.

I realized it was past 10:30. The pictures would be ready by now, and besides, I needed to get over to Tom Augustine's at the Archdiocese to talk to him and the Social Justice Commission group. I put the documents back in my briefcase and made a move.

Driving under swirling, lead-gray skies, I was hit by an idea. From the get-go, I had been thinking that the aid shipment for the junta was less dramatic than the bomb fins that were slated to be shipped to Chile in 1978. Which would make it harder to drum up support. But there was a way to spin it that would create drama.

During this year's presidential campaign, the junta had greatly increased its efforts to terrorize and suppress opposition across El Salvador. And all the aid, except maybe the safety and rescue stuff, would clearly help it reach its goal of total dictatorial rule. But notably, the press was reporting that the junta's big weaknesses were in "command-and-control operations" and "combat counterintelligence." This meant that all the Radio Equipment wouldn't merely help the junta in their routine use of terror: it would drastically increase their power in any new offensive.

The downside of my realization was that if the aid really was as important as I figured, that meant the Carter administration was far less likely to cancel the shipment, given the Reagan transition team about to take over.

I remembered the Thanksgiving Day just passed. The junta's opposition, a broad coalition called the Frente Democrático Revolucionario (Democratic Revolutionary Front) or FDR for short, held an open meeting hosted by the faculty of a famous Jesuit high school in San Salvador. During the meeting, junta troops entered the school and seized and bound the president of the FDR, along with seven Executive Council reps. The next day, they all were found, still bound, having been tortured and killed by gunfire. I grew more anxious. The situation clearly demanded action, but the more I looked at it the less I saw any route to success.

6

I climbed the Archdiocesan steps of the colonial-style brick building and entered the lobby. May Burnet, who worked the switchboard, greeted me with a smile and said the folks in the meeting were eager to hear my news. I walked through a set of wide-open doors into the large wood-paneled conference room. Tom Augustine, tall and dignified, stood and motioned me to a chair next to his. Those attending sat around a long table, with Tom's chair and the one he invited me to take at the center of one of the long sides.

I surveyed the large group gathered around the table, many of them clergy. One woman at the table, youthful with her jet-black hair stylishly cropped—someone I hadn't seen before—drew my attention. She wore a black turtleneck sweater and a small wooden cross on a loop of braided string. I wondered who she was. After taking what I needed from my briefcase, I got settled and shot a questioning look to Tom as he took his seat.

"Ready to go?" he asked. Receiving my assent, he described to those assembled what I had learned this morning: weapons of war, destined for the repressive junta of El Salvador, sat on a San Francisco dock, ready to be loaded and shipped.

But, before signaling to me to begin, he gestured to the woman I had noticed and said he wanted to introduce her to a "dear and honored guest." He gestured in my direction, saying, "Brother Steve Morrow, this is Sister Catherine Ann, a Maryknoller who just returned last night from El Salvador."

Sister Catherine and I exchanged smiles. She was about thirty.

In addition to the black turtleneck, she wore distressed Levi's, hiking boots, and a worn down red parka. She carried a rucksack of faded green. She had a beautiful, warm smile.

Tom then addressed the group. He said that, although most knew what he would say, he had to repeat it before he called on me. He described some events, beginning in 1978, when my union, the ILWU, refused to load bomb fins for the fascist Pinochet regime.

"This union of dockers has a distinguished history in the struggle for social justice, beginning in 1935 with a refusal to load copper, nickel, and brass for the Mussolini war-machine that had invaded Ethiopia."

He then invited me to speak. I stood up and gave them all the low-down on everything I had learned over the course of my action-packed morning. I concluded by stating that the union couldn't by itself make the government change its mind. And because that was so, and considering Reagan's politics, community support would be essential. I then asked if anyone had any comments or questions. Father Robert McGinnis, head of the Archdiocesan staff in San Francisco and chair of its Justice Commission, raised his hand.

"So, the bottom line is that we're talking about building support for your refusal to load the arms—that means publicly announced support, right?"

"Yes, that's right."

"And given the lack of attention for the junta in the press and general public, we need support from what has become, at least to me, the only consistently promising group in the social justice effort: religious groups."

"Yes. Especially since the junta killed the archbishop, we believe religious support for our action might give the powers that be a reason to change their mind. But from that core base, we need to spark a wider public support."

"And what happens if the union doesn't manage to garner that support by the time it announces its refusal?"

"The PCMA would call our hand, and the plan would unravel. If we lose even a round or two of this fight, even if the government wanted to reverse itself it would no longer have the public support to do so."

"So you'll have to announce the refusal before the *Tropic Moon* returns from Seattle to give the government time to go back on its decision. What would be the most effective way to do that?"

"Our thinking is, if the union and those who support us held a media event at the union's offices, it might generate enough support to change the government's mind."

Smiling with approval, Father McGinnis said, "The focus would be on the union, flanked, visually and literally, by representatives of the religious community in their sundry vestments."

At this point my good pal Minister John Boyer, who was on the staff of the World Council of Churches, raised his hand.

"We could best achieve the effect we want to the media by bestowing a blessing for righteousness. In other words, the dockers who refused to load weapons are 'blessed' for their trouble. We could even hold a service that same night."

He had to pause there because of the stir and commotion his idea caused. Good old Johnny always had an eye for drama. The room revved up with excitement when he added, "We could hold the service at the Local 10 hiring hall!"

"Would that be big enough?"

"It's pretty darn big," I assured them. "If we used the balcony and set up the ground floor fully with folding chairs, it could seat well over a thousand."

My mind racing as I envisioned how the whole thing would look on TV, I continued: "We'll erect a fold-up stage, four feet high and thirty feet wide, and get a podium and a sound system. We could lead a big procession into the main hall, a march of a thousand people. Then the speakers proceed onto the stage while everyone else takes their seat."

My description was met with murmurs of agreement. Reverend Carl Merton, director of the lay staff of the Episcopalian Archdiocese of California, piped up over the din. "One more thing, Brother Morrow. The support you're trying to gain with this event—do you mean purely moral and political support, or financial support as well?"

"Let's get something straight here. The union has an absolute rule that we pay as we go. *We* pay for what *we* do. It helps keep us honest."

There was a muted chuckle at my comment. Reverend Merton shot back: "But then the union, by its refusal, would be at risk financially. No matter what support you gain, if this goes on too long, you could be done in in no time."

"That is correct."

"Well then why, pray, are you planning to continue your refusal into a court of law when you'd be certain to lose?"

"Because some fights are too important to give up on. God knows the people on Reagan and the junta's side won't give up, so we can't either. The further we go, the more support we gain, the more we expose this government for who they really care about. Maybe if enough people see that, they'll be forced to reverse their decision."

Tom took the floor then to suggest we take a forty-five-minute break for what he called a light repast. This brought smiles all around, and we started making our way into the dining room.

7

Upon entering the dining room, we were met with a banquet table lined with shrimp and crab salad, French bread, green and black olives, cottage cheese and what seemed like every vegetable under the sun. Tom's idea of a "light repast"! I took my tray of rations but didn't stick around to chat, there was still work to do.

I brought my tray into a temporary office Tom had set up for me and called the union. Shirley Baxter, a mainstay at the union's office, picked up the line. She said that the only caller for me was Doug Martin, the clerk down at Pier 50, who'd said he'd like me to call as soon as possible.

"Damn." I felt the rush of a sick feeling I always get when I know there's bad news. I asked Shirley to put in a call to Brother Jack Mahoney, a friend of mine and the president of Local 19 in Seattle, and get an ETA for the *Moon*'s arriving back in San Francisco.

"Got it. Anything else?"

"Well, you'd best remind him that this is on the quiet."

"Okay. If you're up to tricks again, I'll call and then forget it, too."

"Thanks, Shirley. And tell Jack I'll call him tonight or tomorrow, okay?"

"Sure thing."

Next, I called the officers of our International. I'd delayed calling, knowing they were getting back from an L.A. trip at noon. I soon heard the gruff voice of Brother Joe Margolis, an ILWU vice-president, on the other end of the line. I told him I needed to meet with him and the rest of the International officers. He said he was just about to go for lunch with Paul Murphy, our president, and asked if I could come in around four.

"Sure, that's okay with me."

"Great, but how about also saying what you have in mind? Murphy'll want to know."

The fact is, I didn't really want to field the barrage of questions sure to come my way if I explained it right then.

"Oh, for Christ's sake. I'm down in the trenches and have no time, even for a bite to eat, let alone a horn or two of beer, so please tell Murphy to trust me."

"Okay, but he'll just say that trusting types don't last."

"Well, he ought to know, as a real expert at 'lasting.' But just tell him that I'm on to a thing that could be important, even to you."

I always kidded Joe, but this time he didn't seem to be taking it too well.

"Jesus, okay," he replied in a flat voice. "Four o'clock."

"Perfect. But listen up now, Joe. Don't forget your thinking cap."

"I'm thinking already that I just can't wait."

I couldn't resist a parting shot.

"As you're thinking ahead like that, you ought to do as everyone says."

"And what the hell might that be?" said Joe.

"Keep the faith, brother."

Joe hung up with a sigh.

Next I called Doug down at Pier 50. He answered after just one ring, making me certain the news was bad.

"Hey, Steve. I figured you'd call, so I've been standing by."

"What's cooking?" I asked him.

"I've been looking at the paperwork on our little shipment. Everything's still booked to the *Moon*, and it won't be moved, but now there may be a plan to rebook the aid shipment to the *Tropic Star* and to the *Wind*."

The rush in my stomach had been confirmed. Because of our contracts, the only way we could refuse to load the *Star* and the *Wind* would be a wildcat stoppage: a strike *without* the permission of the union.

Doug added: "As you rolled away, I started wondering why this aid is booked only to the *Moon* when the *Star* is arriving earlier and always has space after her L.A. loadout. Same thing with the *Wind*. After nosing around, I learned that they wanted it all on one ship, to ease its motor transport to San Salvador from the Port of Acajutla."

"Okay. I'm writing all this down."

Doug paused a moment so I could keep up.

"So they booked all the cargo to the *Moon* because it has the space. *But*, they made sure to dray it to the same shipyard as the *Star* and the *Wind* so that if needs be they could quickly switch it. Except now it might be even worse, because now, as it turns out, there's going to be more."

"Oh my God. How much more?"

"I haven't found out yet, but they'd be splitting up the existing cargo onto the *Star* and the *Wind* and putting the new stuff on the *Moon*."

"When do you think they might decide?"

"Jesus, Steve, I don't know, there's no way to tell. The government might hold back the paperwork right up to the time when it's ready to sail. Besides, even if I knew right now they had rebooked, our only course of action is to do a wildcat and hope for some support in the press. Right now we're all by ourselves."

I sighed. "You're right."

"You know what though," Doug went on, "if we can get some press on the dock, a wildcat thing by ordinary folks saying 'No way!' as an issue of conscience might actually be a better way to spark a response. So it could be a lot worse."

I hadn't thought of it that way.

"It sure could."

Doug assured me he would continue to serve as a scout on our skirmish line, and we swapped numbers.

"Thanks again, old bud," I said. "Oh, listen, have you got an ETA for *The Star*?

"They haven't posted it, but the ship might tie up on Saturday."

"You mean, *this* Saturday?"

"'Fraid so."

As I hung up I had the gnawing in the pit of my stomach again. Saturday was only three days away, and I didn't know how in hell we could pull off a successful wildcat strike, let alone an entire political campaign, on such short notice.

8

I left the little office Tom had reserved for me and arrived back in the meeting room to find everyone just getting seated to resume. When I took my place, Tom turned to me and suggested I fill in the group on my union's 1978 refusal to load the bomb fins for Pinochet in Chile so we could compare that to our current situation. I had practiced that spiel enough over the years so that I could tell it straight and smooth. I began the tale I had shaped and been involved with, deeply and proudly.

"Events in nineteen seventy-eight began as they did this year: with a call from a docker on the job, a trip to the dock, and taking a covert roll of photos. Now, the aid itself in 1978 was dramatic: twenty-one crates of bomb fin tail assemblies that I photographed, to great advantage, through the slats of their crating. I had gotten the call at 8:00 on the morning of May 23, and I knew, soon after, that the ETA of the vessel involved was the morning of June 2.

"After my trip to that dock in 1978, I saw the brothers who I will see again today after we adjourn: the International officers of my union, the ILWU. Throughout the course of our refusal to work the Pinochet arms shipment, those officers and those of Local 10 continued with normal contract talks. Given how completely our daily lives are ruled by our contract, I should note the union's refusal to work during negotiations was unprecedented. I saw the International guys when they broke for lunch, and they began to explore how to get away with a refusal.

"We all wondered where the union possibly could find support for its refusal. Recall that Congress had been hesitant about granting aid to Pinochet, who had slaughtered many during his 1973 coup. Opposition to him increased, later, when Congress learned that the CIA had helped to topple and kill Allende, the Chilean socialist President. Given the strikes against Pinochet in Chile and the suppression that followed, in June 1976 Congress passed an embargo against military aid to Pinochet. The Carter Administration, which was beginning a policy tilt toward human rights, pressured Pinochet to stop the repression and produce a report on the 'disappeared.'

"The Congressional embargo of 1976 had not extended, however, to arms already in the pipeline at the time of its passage in the Congress. So, even in May, 1978, Pinochet was still due to get a hundred million dollars' worth of military assistance. To us in the union, however, and to a whole lot of folks, that was completely unacceptable.

"The union had been condemning the coup in Chile and the death of President Allende since 1973. We supported the efforts of Congress and others to learn the role of the CIA in the coup. At our union's biennial convention in 1977 we urged Carter to impose a total boycott on Chile. We supported the arms embargo–while pointing out its huge loophole–and endorsed the Chilean people's marches and fasting for the 'disappeared.'

"Because we reported on these issues and our position in our union newspapers, by 1978 most of our members believed that we ought to do what we could to put an end to Pinochet. So, when the fins showed up, we dusted off what we'd been saying for a long time and set about getting support.

"We decided to announce our refusal on May 31, giving the Carter administration three days to back off and us ten days to build support. With the clock ticking, we started calling those in Congress we had supported and who had also been keeping a close watch on Pinochet. I should note that given the current political climate, I suspect that such moves would be less successful now than in 1978."

I paused to give an opportunity for questions or comments, but everyone seemed eager to keep listening. I continued:

"We knew by the morning of May 31 that at least a dozen members of the House, along with several senators, would speak on our behalf. We thought that was a pretty fair start, so at four that afternoon I informed the steamship line and the stevedore firm, and through them, the PCMA and the government, that we would refuse to load the fins.

"By then, we had worked out a good way to make a public refusal. I have an old friend I can trust who's a byline reporter on city news and feature stories for the *Examiner.* I filled him in on what might come down, since an in-depth story ready to go would help all around. Because I had the snaps, paperwork and all the rest ready, he immediately saw a great story. We met with my pal's city editor on Saturday, May 27, to bring him up to date and read a draft of the story. The three of us also met on Monday morning, May 29, with the *Examiner* publisher, whom everyone seemed to call, affectionately, the young Willie Hearst. Our meeting ended with a decision: barring another quake, on June 4, we would have the front-page headline story.

"Everything was ready to go. But then on June 1 the stevedore called to say the ship had been sent to a yard and wouldn't arrive for twelve days. The fins would be drayed–that is, moved from the dock that day, but to an unknown destination. We began to scratch our heads.

"On June 10, the fins showed up at the Oakland Army Terminal, booked to a government charter ship with an ETA from Guam on Sunday, June 25. And I learned that the ship, having been diverted here from the last leg of its regular run from Galveston to the Pacific, would drop the aid in Panama for subsequent shipment to Chile. That the shipment had been on a public dock and booked to a public carrier, had given us an opportunity. The Oakland Army terminal, by contrast, could keep the press away from the ship. Given our refusal to load the arms, they might even employ civil service dockers from its next-door neighbor, the Naval Supply Depot.

"On Sunday, June 18, the *Chronicle-Examiner* gave us a great front-page headline: 'DOCKERS HALT BOMBS TO CHILE'.

"Now, Senator Ted Kennedy had advised some folks that on the nineteenth he'd be making a Senate speech on Chilean issues, and we knew that if we had announced our refusal by then, he would surely commend us. Sure enough, he did precisely that— and his speech gave us really good press. With a vessel then steaming for Oakland, the timing gave the press something it really likes: an unfolding story. It was picked up by the UP, AP, and Reuters and printed, sometimes with my photo, in the next day's *New York Times*, *Los Angeles Times*, *Washington Post*, *Boston Globe*, *Chicago Tribune*, *Seattle Times*, and *Wall Street Journal*. It went on to appear in every country in North, Central, and South America— except Chile—and all over Europe.

"Then the Pentagon made a big mistake. On Monday, saying that the fins were for practice bombs, it couldn't understand the fuss and announced it had no plans to review the shipment. That story, with its dismissive comment, aroused wide-spread indignation. The *Washington Post* reported 'the fuss' the next day and mentioned that the Department of State was saying privately that 'the wisdom of going ahead' with the shipment was 'slated for a full and complete review.' Our allies working in Washington really moved it along.

"Right at 8:00 on Friday morning, an office staffer told me the person at the State Department in charge of reviewing the shipment to Chile was on the line, and she was anxious to speak to me. I was anxious in turn, until I heard the friendly southern voice of Patricia Derian, one of the good ones. As Assistant Secretary of State for Human Rights, she had helped fashion the current Carter tilt towards human rights.

"Derian got right to the point: the shipment had been canceled. Pending a full and complete review, she said, the rest of the Pinochet pipeline also would be on indefinite hold. And the US Ambassador to Chile, George Landau, was being brought back to report and advise on all matters. She then explained that she had wanted to call earlier but couldn't do so until she had addressed the media. Even then, she could just squeeze in a call, for she was due at the White House. She apologized for being so rushed.

"I thanked her for her call and the good news, and made some of my own calls right away. The first was to my pal at the *Examiner*. Its noon edition on June 23 included a front-page story under the headline 's.f. CHILE PROTEST WINS—ARMY HALTS BOMB PARTS TO CHILE.'"

I concluded by taking a somber stare around the room and saying, "Reagan's election will make it a *lot* harder this time."

Even though I cut my story severely, as always I took too long to tell it. But Tom said it was deeply interesting and asked if there were questions or comments. He recognized Tim Richards, staff chair of the Service Committee of Friends. Tim asked who in Congress had lent support to our cause.

"Because I had no role in putting together Congressional support, I never knew our tally. But I do know that the core supporters consisted of those who had signed a letter to President Carter just after Ms. Derian had met with the press. Our International president, Paul Murphy, received a copy and sent one to each local. I can get you a copy if you'd like."

"That would be a great help," Tim replied. "If the union again refuses to load arms being sent to a dictator, those who stepped forward in 1978 should be advised of this refusal, if only as a courtesy. But even without the change in the political climate, we face a different and far from promising set of congressional factors. When you announced your stance against arms for Pinochet, no fall election campaigns were about to start, and the Congress was on its year-end holiday. What's more, a newly elected president always has a honeymoon of at least three or four months."

Tom Augustine nodded in approval of Tim's remarks, then called on Father Malone. Father Malone reminds me of Pat O'Brien, the movie actor, so seeing him always sends me deep into nostalgia for the Saturday matinees of the late thirties and early forties.

"I want to say first that the fins and the photos of them were dramatic. And together, they explain, at least partly, the media coverage you got. The aid this time—at least in terms of what we know now—is far less dramatic."

That put the movies out of my mind.

"So far, yes," I admitted.

I was about to start on my theory about the radio equipment, but before I could, Father Malone went on: "I'm no student of matters like these, but the shipment could be intended for what is now being talked about as a major escalation. From what I hear and read, the junta lacks exactly the items contained in the shipment– radio sets, monitors and auxiliary items–that could provide the technical means they need to place more troops into the field. In other words, the junta hasn't been able to launch an offensive like the one it is speaking of now for the simple reason that it hasn't had the means to deploy, control, and coordinate the many small units such an offensive would require due to the mountainous and forested terrain. So, if the aid now sitting on the dock were used in this way, we surely would have some drama."

I chuckled in my head. He said it better than I could have. Judging from the nodding heads and agitation of those listening, I could tell his words had had a lot of impact.

Malone continued in his easy manner: "I'm thinking out loud here. If the *Moon* arrives in a little more than three weeks, a press conference could be held on the Monday of Christmas week. That way, we might, to our advantage, project the spirit of the time of year. In the meantime, we should recruit those who support us to send wires endorsing the refusal to load the arms, quietly tipping them off about the union's plan to announce it and the support it would have.

"We might also prepare for a second service down at the dock, perhaps with the *Moon* itself serving as backdrop. In other words, though we can fill in the blanks later, I think our planning should take account of the *Moon*'s departure from here with an ongoing series of events that would heighten the unfolding drama."

Father Malone's ideas were really terrific. I was excited to hear more, but I happened to get beeped at that exact moment. I always tried to answer a beep as soon as I could. You never know what it could be.

9

I smiled to Father Malone in apology for my beeper going off and headed for the office phone, my anxiety rising rapidly. The woman at the answering service gave me some relief when she told me that John Tilby was on the line. John is a steward on Pier 32 who drives shipboard winches. Does a crackerjack job of it, too, and he could more than hold his own with any boss on the front.

"Hey John, what's doing?"

"Brother Steve! Well, we're being asked to use some shot gear here at Pier 32 is what's doing. The ship's supposed to get new falls and heel blocks on every set of gear, and the only gear still waiting on that is the one we're being asked to use. The superintendent says we should use the crappy gear as it is only for what they claim will be six loads. Instead, we said screw that, so now we're standing down. Okay?"

"Yeah, sure. Good work." I was still thinking about the El Salvador issues, but I couldn't let that affect my work as union officer.

"And guess what they're asking us to load! Pallets of four fifty-five-gallon drums of—would you believe it?—parathion concentrate. One drop of that on your skin makes you a vegetable, and they're telling us to load it with bum gear."

"Jesus! Who's the superintendent?"

"Jack Webster."

"And where is he now?"

"He's up on the ship, but if you hold, I'll get him here."

"Okay, but listen, John, you're absolutely right on this one, but

I've got something I've got to finish up. I'll tell Webster to do what you've recommended or it will have to wait to be settled at maybe ten tonight."

"Great, I'll be right back," Tilby replied.

It was five minutes or more before I heard Webster sound his characteristically cheery hello.

"What?"

"Webster, I hear you're wrong again."

"Look, Morrow. The gear will do for just six loads."

"Oh really? Then what are the new falls and blocks on deck for? Decoration?"

"She's got to sail no later than four to keep her berth tomorrow night. And once she gets her cargo, she'll be ready to sail."

"Oh good, at least now I know why the *ship* wants to sail! Look, the contract doesn't speak about gear that will *do*. Now you have three options: either sail away without the stuff, or make the gear safe and go full speed ahead to Long Beach, or stand pat, lose tonight, and then decide tomorrow."

Webster sighed and put me back on to Tilby, who said he'd call me with updates and hung up.

I was about to rejoin the meeting with Father Malone and the others when my beeper went off again. It was Michael McSweeney, the terminal manager at Pier 50, calling about that shipment to Hong Kong aboard the *Astral Tide* that the night workers had refused to load.

"I'm telling you, Morrow, it's a fucking bum beef!"

"Well look, Mike, if you'd like we can lay this whole thing out…in an arbitration."

"We'd like to get this resolved without a pissing contest, if it's all the same to you."

"Pissing isn't really the question here. Anyway, whatever you've got in mind, it can't be today or tomorrow."

"But we've got to get this settled! Christ, we aren't even asking these guys for what they get paid to do."

"Wait, so the boxes went back to the dock? Is the ship gone?"

"She sailed just now. We've got to stay on schedule."

Perfect. I faked a disappointed sigh and said, "Dammit. If the ship's gone, there's not much for me to take a look at. If only you had called me this morning…"

"But I was told you were tied up in a deposition!"

"Mike, how are you going to resolve a thing when we can't even see it?"

"Look, let me just take a look. Maybe I… yes! There's a sister ship coming in Monday morning, exactly the same specs as the *Tide*."

"That might be okay, but with the things I've got in my book, I'll have to call you back."

"Hey, now, wait a minute, Morrow. I've been here since two and, as I said, this whole damn thing is a total shit show."

"Hey, Mike, slow down. I'm trying to work this out. So, how about my putting you on hold and making a call, you know, to see if I can rearrange?"

"Ugh, fine." I checked the time then and saw that it was 2:20. I paid a quick visit to the can, had a pissing contest of my own, and got back to the phone.

"Jesus, Mike. I'm really screwed. At least now, there's just no way."

"Look, just work it out and call me at home."

"What time?"

"Oh, for Christ's sake. You'll call whenever you damn well please, like you always do."

"I'm asking that so as not to disturb you."

"Oh, Jesus. Look, I've been disturbed—no fucking end to it— since two in the goddamn morning, and this is not helping me one damn bit. So, do me the favor of hanging up and calling me tonight."

"No problem. But listen, Mike, you need sleep. And a couple of stiff horns of beer."

"You're saying that as what? An old pal?"

"Yeah. I know over the years we've had our rounds and all that, but you're not actually the worst of the lot."

"Look, just give me a call at my abode."

"Sure. But don't forget, sleep and a few horns!" I smiled when I heard the click ending our call.

They were just rounding up the meeting when I got back. Tom looked around, smiled, tapped the table, and cleared his throat.

"Before we close, I should ask if there is anything else for Steve."

Someone down the back asked how much time we'd have once we announced the refusal.

"We'll have about two days before we have to go to arbitration. Then another two days before we have to arbitrate for a second and final time and, finally, another two before we get hauled into court."

We agreed to plan events between each series of arbitration. These would start locally, but we could hopefully get them to spread all along the West Coast and then the whole country. We agreed to meet the following Wednesday at 9:00 and to stay, if possible, as late as 4:00 pm. Tom thanked everybody for attending and then invited Father McGinnis, whom he described as "my mentor, friend and boss," to close out the meeting. Father McGinnis smiled and surveyed the room, a determined look in his eye.

"On behalf of the Archdiocese, I'll simply echo the thanks from Tom. Now let's get ready for next week."

There was a soft applause. As we left, May Burnet passed out copies of the sign-in sheet and a report on El Salvador. I figured both would come in handy for my upcoming meeting with our union leadership.

10

The traffic was lightening but the mist was only getting darker. I turned into the underground garage beneath our International office over on Franklin at Geary. Pressing four on the elevator, I ascended from the dark shadows of the eerie basement up to the modern trimmings of the International's roost. I walked over to the reception desk. Betsy Palmer, the receptionist, greeted me with a smile.

"They're waiting for you in Paul's office—but I also have a message for you."

John Tilby had called from Pier 32. The ship, with nothing done about the gear and nothing further to do, had sailed at 3:15. I thanked Betsy and made my way through the corridor, passing a dramatic series of enlarged black-and-white photographs of life and work on the waterfront.

ILWU International President Paul Murphy's office door was almost always wide open, and Paul, as usual, immediately smiled and nodded to me. Our president's office was fitted out like something on the *Queen Elizabeth*. The *original* one. He occupied an old brown leather chair behind a well-ordered oak desk that stretched across the corner of the room above the intersection of Franklin and Geary. His chair had a high back and padded arm rests, a tad worn, but still serviceable, like the deck of a fine old ship. When I came in the room, I saw his crew seated in front of his desk in equally handsome brown leather easy chairs. A couch and two oak end tables were placed along the two walls that faced Paul's desk. On each end table sat a brass ashtray and a brass reading lamp with a frosted chimney and a green glass shade.

Like all the offices, this one was carpeted in brown and had off-white walls and cream drapes. On the walls hung an old polished-brass ship's clock and barometer, along with four large paintings of sailing ships bounding through troubled seas, with canvas sails flying; some old, framed charts of West Coast ports; and a wheel made from the wood of an ash tree.

As almost always, there were good vibes in Paul's office. I raised a hand and laughed, telling the crew to be at ease and not to get up. I shook hands with VP Joe Margolis, who seemed as salty as he was on the phone, Bill Hanson, another ILWU vice-president, and Pete Turner, our secretary-treasurer. Paul nodded to me as he talked into the phone, saying, "I'll call back in an hour or so."

I thought to myself, *These are good guys; always ready to hear from down below.*

Paul hung up the phone, waved me a jovial salute, and got straight to the point.

"Well, here we go—but where are we?"

"There's military hardware on 50-D, slated for the junta down in El Salvador. I got us a copy of all the paperwork and five sets of snaps."

Once I had said it, Paul dropped his smile, tilted back in his chair, pursed his lips and snorted, "I don't suppose you have anything like your snaps of the fins in 1978."

"No, 'fraid not. But there is a way of seeing that what I've got could be darn good. I'll get to that. But let's start off with the notes I took while I waited for the snaps."

Paul scanned the four brief pages and, passing them to Bill, glanced at the snaps. Paul frowned at the images: "What's this 'safety and rescue' stuff?"

"I don't know. Tom Augustine at the Archdiocese called a friend back east who studies the foreign aid budget for the Conference of Catholic Bishops. He's going to get more information on the shipment. So, if you ask Marty to get on it, maybe he should start by phoning Tom." Marty Duval made up our one-person research staff.

Paul wrote a note as he said, "Yeah, right," and soon passed the pages to the crew.

"Why the *Moon*?"

I said I didn't know and passed on what Doug had said about the possibility of it getting switched onto the *Star* and the *Wind,* with the *Star* possibly arriving on Saturday. Just three days away.

Paul immediately cut to what was next: "And what do we do if it *is* Saturday?"

"Well, taking into account the things we've already said about the junta being so brutal, then maybe some of our members pull a wildcat and walk off the pier, while declaring their actions as individual moral decisions in order to shield the union. And after declaring our solidarity with the murdered Archbishop Romero, buy more time to build more support."

"How?"

"Those involved could say to the press that, because they believed that this aid was immoral, they walked off the job. And the move by the PCMA to force the dockworkers to do what they saw as wrong was immoral, too. With halfway decent press, things like that could get support. And with weekend work from the hiring hall being all voluntary and keeping our ranks up to date, our refusal could get us to the close of the Monday morning job dispatch without an arbitration."

"Okay," Paul said. "Let's go on to where we might stand otherwise. Any speakers?"

Joe Margolis frowned and, in a growl, asked me to identify the pal I had been working with. I told him it was pier clerk Doug Martin, adding that someone from the warehouse division like Joe probably wouldn't know Doug. Joe turned to Paul, who reassured him: "Martin's okay, so, no problem there."

Joe seemed almost disappointed, like he was looking to catch me on something. "Okay," was all he said.

Next, Paul asked if I had seen the religious people. I told him that I had, "just as we had agreed." From one of my folders, I dug out the sign-in sheet, which also included those who had not attended. Now that we had a plan, I would be keeping notes on such things so that if asked, I could make a decent report. And I'd keep those notes, as I had done with those on the Pinochet aid and a few other such matters I had worked on, in manila folders with one for every day the issue remained in play.

"Most of those folks were at the Archdiocesan building for a post-election talk on what to do now," I explained, handing the sign-in sheet to Paul. "That was lucky for me because, when I walked in, the group gave me the chance to talk. You'll see, as in the past, the group is broad and impressive."

Paul smiled: "This is really something."

Secretary-Treasurer Pete agreed: "This list keeps growing all the time."

Then Joe, who hated religion of all kinds, started in on me again. "What'd you tell the group?"

By this time I had warmed to getting Joe riled up, so I just said, "Don't worry Joe, I didn't tell them any precious secrets or anything."

As I tried to fill them in on the meeting, Joe cut me off: "You know, Morrow, you really are something else. I mean, you were detailed to do this work, but here you are, having upset us all again with your kidding and fooling. And actually, this is without a doubt your modus operandi. And, though I hate to say it, no grown man would kid like this."

I took Joe's comments in good spirit. "Okay, okay, I give up."

And at that, everyone had a laugh. Then Paul urged the group to hush, looking almost fatherly as he quieted everyone with a gesture. "So, what really happened?" he asked.

I read them my notes from the meeting, explaining how I'd asked those present to support our refusal to load the arms.

Turning to Paul, I went on: "As we've done in the past, I like the idea of getting started with a jointly called press conference in the big room we use for such events. There, we would announce our refusal, and they would read statements in support. If they have enough lead time, they said that they could hand out wires received from all over in support of our action."

Our union VP Bill Hanson piped up, saying that he wanted to confirm that everyone there understood that the union's refusal, addressed to the government, would not be a legal act.

"Yes, that's right."

"And the people at the Archdiocese would support our refusal."

"Yeah, at least the ones who spoke."

"And they also know that, given the back to the Cold War, screw human rights campaign Reagan ran on, things could get rough, right?"

"I told them the union would face heavy fines. The government might seize all our assets and..." Turning to Paul, I added, "They will surely jail our union leaders."

"Hey, don't look at me," said Paul, "You'll be in the next cell!" He was serious, but kept a twinkle in his eyes.

Bill turned to Pete Turner, our secretary-treasurer. Because Pete was a man who focused on detail, I thought the discussion would be sidetracked. Sure enough, the next question seemed to digress: "So, how did they view a media thing?"

I was not sure what he meant by *media thing*, but said that they wanted to do a blessing of the dockers. "Everyone bought the image of the docker who says 'no' to junta aid but also gets blessed for his trouble."

Pete grinned. "There's nothing like that in all of U.S. history!"

"Talk about hitting the ground running!" Bill chimed in.

Joe asked me where they would give this blessing of theirs, "up on the hill of St. Mary's?"

My answer brought him up short: "Well, they talked about using our hiring hall. Having lined up in our lobby, they'd get to our stage and the first row of chairs after coming down the center aisle in their robes of office. They'd begin with all the stir and color of a procession, down through our assembled ranks, families and friends."

That stunned everyone to silence. This was broken by Paul, who shot up from his chair and slammed his hands down on the desk. The chair fired back and smacked against the corner wall.

"*Genius!*" he cried with a lively grin. The other guys echoed his enthusiasm.

"They sure as hell got show biz down," Joe conceded.

"That's some image," Bill agreed.

"Dockers and clergy, side by side, the place completely jammed," Pete added, mesmerized.

"As for me, I don't like their shows of hocus-and-pocus," Joe remarked. "All their stuff is 'pie-in-the-sky-by-and-by' to cloud folks' thinking. So, whatever they did in your hall, it would be a show biz thing, in no way different from what they've been pulling since Adam and Eve. But with the repression and terror, I'd have to go along with it all. In other words, as for my religious skepticism, I would have no choice but to rise above them."

We were aware of his carrying on and realized that he got a kick from that, and we knew that a quick shake of the head and a faint smile would let him know his message got through. He may have said all that tongue in cheek, but it was hard not to laugh when a curmudgeonly guy like Joe Margolis claimed he had 'risen above' the Church.

Joe continued: "I'll go along with their circus so long as this is understood: when a fakir shows up in his velvet robes and a great big hat, I won't kneel. And I won't kiss rings or sing some screwy hymn." Joe could barely hold himself in as he finished. Although he was in no way to be trifled with, he also loved to sound the trumpet and charge the barricades. He was a complex guy who would kid himself as he was kidding you.

Paul answered for all of us when he said, "No problem there."

Once he'd heard that, Joe flashed us his Yogi Berra grin, feigned a punch, and got himself aboard, saying, "And the TV folks, meanwhile, would be cranking away, so you guys got it right: we'd hit the track at a good clip by getting a bunch of fakirs to put on a show in the hiring hall."

Paul looked around at all the smiles and, to rein us in, announced that it was 4:45, and he had to make some calls. He sent everyone off to "do what you've got to do until, say, 5:30."

There were nods of agreement all around. Joe said, "I've got plenty to do, Lord knows, but I'm not going to get cut off. And that's because I just don't like leaving things only partly said. So, I'll go along, but I've got no liking for the hocus-pocus of this world and want my objections recorded. So, if you please, brother Turner."

Pete shrugged, smiled and said, as Paul had, "No problem." We then recessed.

I also needed to make some calls, so I headed for a room kitty-corner to Paul's office that had six cubicles for those in need of a phone and desk. I walked down the hall to that room, past old oak and glass bookcases displaying objects from the union's history, including models of ships of every use and propulsion that are real works of art. On the walls were more memorabilia, everything from old handheld cargo hooks affixed to varnished hatch boards, framed headlines and articles, columns and editorials, clippings of *Shipping News*, campaign ads and obits, typed and handwritten letters, cables and telegrams, first-draft notes and printed copies of speeches, handbills, leaflets, bulletins, election placards and picket signs, posters and buttons and arm bands and photographs of dockers throughout the union history. There were even paintings of four ILWU members who had been killed in Spain fighting on behalf of the socialist government during its civil war in the 1930s.

It was enough to make a fella well up at the best of times, but today it felt especially poignant.

11

I called Shirley at the local's office. She said she had bad news and, after a pause, told me someone had been hurt. Apparently while working steel coils, a brother had fallen nine feet or so, breaking a cheekbone, collarbone, wrist, forearm, and ankle. That was bad enough but, because he had fallen into a deep wing of one of the holds where coils were stowed, he had to be hoisted out and brought to the dock in a basket. It took his gang over an hour to do that.

I have to say that injuries are the only thing I haven't missed since I said good-bye to my job on the waterfront to work as a union officer. The injury doesn't need to involve a friend or someone you like. Just knowing that one of the gang has been hurt takes a toll. In the worst case, having to pay final respects is about the saddest, toughest thing a docker does.

Shirley promised to get me the phone numbers I'd need the next day to follow-up, then filled me in on a job walkout at pier 27. When fumes had built up during a discharge of cars in a ship at the dock, two decks already having been discharged, the folks unlashing cars had asked for a carbon monoxide test. The company rep told them that he had no testing meter, a clear violation of the contract. Now, everyone had seen his meter case, which had three or four meters and dozens of tubes, a million times. And the explanation he gave for this?

"Probably one of the dockers stole it."

"Un-believable."

I shook my head in disbelief and called Fred Darwin, the

union steward for pier 27. Fred told me the supervisor claimed that someone had stolen the testing meters to set him up for a walkout as revenge for a beef he had won two weeks earlier. Bottom line, his whole story was far out, and he hadn't a shred of evidence for it. Clearly the guy had forgotten his meter case and was trying to cover his ass. That rep then compounded his claim with another insulting one: the fumes were "not that bad."

If the boss couldn't ensure the fumes had not reached toxic levels, the workers could not be expected to work. He had shown contempt for the workers, the union and the contract, and I would write a claim for a full day's pay.

When that matter was taken care of, I touched base with Tom Augustine at the San Francisco Archdiocese. I got right to my point, saying, "the earlier meeting was dynamite. The guys up here have bought the package and are on board with the plan for a blessing. But we haven't gotten around to discussing the climate. I reckon they might say the dockers should stage the walkout as an individual moral statement, possibly even before the tally. It's best to advise all hands about that possibility, even if only in passing."

I'd been wanting to get to that so neither he nor anyone else would be surprised by a caper on Saturday. I was speaking indirectly, because I hadn't been able to share all the information, but I saw no better way.

Tom immediately said, "Yeah, okay. I think the folks who were here today would approve. The conversation today made that clear. Some of us are already seeing El Salvador as another potential Vietnam."

Tom explained to me that in the latest *Examiner* there was a piece on the foreign aid bill the House passed late yesterday that was eerily familiar.

"Speak of the shades of Vietnam!"

"What does the piece say?"

"First, that U.S. funds can no longer be used for land reform. Nor can they be used, and I quote, 'to nationalize the economy'. Even though both those things have only strengthened the right! Second, U.S. training of foreign troops will no longer include required courses on human rights. Such courses have never been more than window dressing in the past, but now even that halfhearted pretense will be eliminated."

"Jesus Christ." I said I'd call him tonight and we hung up.

I got back to the meeting with my union leadership. Paul began by saying, having given some thought to how we might start our media event, he liked it even better. But he wanted to confirm if we still felt as we had before the break. When we all did so, he made a motion to mark off the matter, saying, "If the principals now buy in, and we opt for a refusal, we'll go with what Steve has reported." Again, everyone gave an enthusiastic yes. Paul turned to me, saying, "And you'll meet on Wednesday."

"Yeah, right. And I left it as I said I would: we've got to know what they can and will do for us."

"And what they'll take to their members is what we just went over?" said Paul.

"At least, to start with. They also talked about things they could do to follow up before and during any court proceedings. And they talked of escalating if things went the contract route."

"Okay, good. And how about a date for our announcement of a 'no'?"

"Until we have a firm ETA and know the details of the ship, that question cannot be answered. But as I said when starting off, it will be some three to four weeks before the *Moon* gets back here, unless they choose to load this Saturday on the *Tropic Star* and the *Wind*. They ended by saying that they hoped for a resolution by the Monday of Christmas week, that week having a flavor all its own."

Paul was good at keeping the ball rolling. He moved things on to questions of which ship the cargo would be loaded onto, saying, "The bottom line, at least for now, is that the shipper's options– the *Tropic Moon* or the *Star* and the *Wind*– are both open to them. Both have been staged on paper, and either could receive new cargo up to her sailing time. But since for both we've got a weekend, it would be Monday at the earliest before you had to arbitrate."

"Right on all counts," I said.

"And if you got charged with disrupting the job dispatch because you advised folks of the beef, you could say to the press that the refusal to take the job was equivalent to refusing to do work on the ship in two ways: the refusals were completely spontaneous and showed the ranks to be well informed."

"Hey, that's pretty good, old bub," I said.

"Feel free to use it, then."

"Don't worry, I will. And by pressing the point that the actions were matters of conscience for those on the job, we'd have accumulated at least some local support by noon, Sunday. But we should also be ready to argue for the refusal as a moral issue. A matter of conscience."

I saw that Pete was ready to leave, but I still needed him for something.

"Another thing: Tom Augustine and his colleagues would like to know what we have said about the junta's reign of terror."

Paul, knowing how much work it would entail to pull together the information requested, deferred to Pete, who said, "Sure. And I'd be getting to that on our own account, too. So, say we begin with the latest thing from the Executive Board?"

Because Pete was mostly asking me, I responded: "We got your phone memo on that, but we don't have the minutes, or at least I haven't seen them."

"We had to check out an item with brother Takara, and the minutes would have been signed only late Friday, but you ought to get them today. And as we said on the phone, the Exec Board's latest on El Salvador will be in our next *Dispatcher* (The ILWU Newspaper). Our masthead date is Friday, but printing starts tonight. If it's the *Star*, you'll have plenty of copies. The issue will repeat what we said when Archbishop Romero was killed. And maybe the story we've been hoping to finish, on the murders of the FDR people. As for that, we've decided on an approach and have gotten a start, but right now, no one knows who did that job."

"Hold on!" I got out the report May had given us at the meeting and showed it around. Its title read: "The FDR Murders: The Witness of the Church."

I passed the document to Pete, who scanned over it.

"What does it say?" Joe asked.

"I didn't have time to give it a close reading, but it says that troops of the National Guard were fully responsible."

"You've got to be kidding."

"No, really. Its primary source is the Human Rights Commission of the Church of El Salvador."

"I'll be a son of a bitch. That's amazing, considering that the report comes from the church."

I should explain. When the FDR Executive Council were slaughtered, the junta blamed a "death squad," to avoid any interruption in aid received from the United States. But because its self-interest was so clear, nobody bought that story. The Jesuit host of the FDR meeting said that the guests were bound and taken away by uniformed troops of the National Guard. But the junta's small, wealthy civilian party, the Christian Democrats, denied this. With their leader, Napoleón Duarte, putting that line out and getting major play in the media, a lot of folks in Washington got on the fence, claiming to be confused. But here was a church commission report that clearly declared the troops of the junta— armed by the United States of America—had committed the exact kind of heinous crime Romero had warned about.

The others might have been less surprised than Joe—at least they claimed so—but they seemed pleased as they looked over the pages passed to them. They all began to say how the commission report would really help.

After Pete said we'd each get a copy of the commission's report, Bill took the floor, and I'll be darned if he didn't say what Father Malone had: "With the items we now have to draft, we'll have to discuss such things, but until then here are a couple things to mull over. The FDR murders have to be viewed as a prelude to the junta's promised offensive. But to mount that, it also needs what already is staged on 50-D, because, despite all the aid it has already received, it needs that radio stuff for battle command and control. So to me, at least, aid like this seems to be a move, as in Vietnam in 1963, toward the US intervening with troops."

The others might have been thinking along the same lines because they were all visibly sobered. Bill turned to me, asking whether similar views had been expressed at Tom's. I said yes and explained. After a brief pause, Paul asked me whether Tom and his group wanted anything else from the union. I said that, after hearing my explanation of 1978, they wanted to see the letter we had sent Carter briefing him on the support we had received in the Congress. Pete said that it wouldn't take long for him to do that since Marty and his folks would help, and he promised me five sets of the paperwork for the snaps.

Pete left to get to work, and Paul proceeded: "Maybe we should now touch on another question: what do we do if after our refusal, we see no blinking at all, or if they stare back and reject our refusal? Steve, did Tom and his folks discuss that?"

I said they had and that they also had some plans in mind if that happened. Joe thumped the arm of his easy chair and smiled broadly. "Don't tell me they also talked about a way for us to sound off and then beat a retreat?!"

"Maybe they could arrange a wrinkle or two before conceding?" Paul said.

"So, what would they do as we're about to be laid to rest—read that psalm about the valley of death?" said Joe.

I could see that Joe was having his fun but, because I also had to get things straight, I changed the tone.

"Before we get to that, I'd have to give you the lead-in, okay? So, I took them through the contract, all right?"

Paul chimed in: "They know that, according to the contract, if we refused to continue the work, we could quickly be forced into line, right? So, they also know that their support would be key, from start to finish. So, first, a media event and then a blessing, and there could be more."

"Right." I took them through the time frame of events our friends in the Church had in mind.

Paul leaned back in his chair. "These folks are something else."

"How would word of our refusal start to spread, Steve?" Bill asked.

"With our okay and as much lead time as we could provide, wires in support of the dockers' walkout would arrive from all over the place, and copies of them would be handed out at the media event. Wires from L.A. and Seattle, Tacoma, and Portland, with our okay, might be followed by supporting events in those regions that would also be coordinated with our longshore locals. And I told them that to get ready for what we might need, you guys would get the locals on board.

"After the blessing, they'd continue beating the bushes for supporters among the religious and clergy. And as they garnered more support, they would keep us up to date so that you could advise the PCMA and, thus, the government."

As I laid out the whole thing, I started to think this plan might actually come together. Pete came back through the door.

"Marty's on board. He'll have the papers ready for us by the time we're ready to quit. But here are the items they've already copied." He gave the crew copies of the report I'd shown them, and I got back my originals.

Paul, in closing the meeting, began to summarize: "We've always known that we can get clobbered even when we have a really good issue and make first-rate moves. So, with the aid on Pier 50 and the *Star* possibly arriving on Saturday, *just three days from now*, we'll begin to weigh the risks that any refusal will entail. And we need to reconsider our assumption that we could always back off from a refusal, if need be, and remain unified. With Romero killed, we can no longer make that assumption.

"But we can assume that the Reaganites are already pushing for more aid, and that they could view Carter's backing off as an opportunity to test us again. They could decide to move right away, hoping to get what they really want most when it comes to unions: a full-blown confrontation, defined and made decisive by their cold war thinking. They might even take a swipe at American workers and unions who support a refusal—for example, by going to Congress and asking for legislation to make it a crime to interfere with a shipment of this sort."

"They might even get that passed," I added.

"I believe this junta aid was sent to us by the Reagan team as payback, not just for the union's refusal to handle an arms shipment destined for Pinochet, but for a whole lot of other things that go much further back."

Everything he said sobered me. Especially that theory.

"This has been a good talk, men, but I've got to go. Good night."

We all exchanged anxious smiles and worried frowns, considering what we might face over the three days leading up to Saturday.

I passed Betsy's desk on the way out. There, on the phone, was Joe Margolis. As I drew near, he raised a hand, cupped the phone, and said, "Good report there, soldier."

Like I said, a complex guy. Made me feel a little easier.

But not too much.

12

Through a night of heavy traffic and rain, I headed for what has been my home for almost three years, an apartment on the top floor of a four-story building on North Point. I moved here in September 1978, after I lost my wife of less than five years. She was an organizer on the regional staff of AFSCME (the American Federation of State, County, and Municipal Employees). One day she took a long drive north to meet some folks at Sonoma State University. Coming back late on a stormy night not unlike tonight, she was hit by a big rig on Route 101. I miss her a lot.

To cut down on my thinking about our lives together, I moved from our rented place on Potrero Hill, only a block from where I'd grown up, and found a new place. It was close to work.

The move helped a lot. After a year or so, I was regaining a social life, going back to the places I had once known and the things I had done. My wife and I had done pretty well together. I didn't go looking for a life of ladies, wine and song, but I was beginning to think about moving on. Slowly.

I opened the door to my empty home. I checked the mail–a fishing tackle catalogue–left my briefcase on the table and hung up my jacket, a dark blue plaid Filson. I strolled over to my window and scanned the view from the Presidio to the Golden Gate. Sausalito, Tiburon, Angel Island, and finally, Alcatraz, stretching eastward between the north end of the Berkeley hills. The dark fog of the coming storm cast a haze over the whole dark image, making everything less clear.

I fixed myself a vodka on the rocks and settled on the couch, my back to the storm, to make some calls. I began with the answering service and said that I was going off page and would be at home. Learning that Charlie Wilson, the union's nighttime business agent, was home on page, I said I'd call at five in the morning to go on page. I called Tom Augustine and heard his office tape say that he was at a meeting but thought he'd be back home—or back in his office, again, at about 10:00.

Next, I called Nick Rowan, the steward for the *Tide* who first told me about the arms shipment on pier 50. His wife told me that he was out for choir practice.

"Excuse me?" I had seen often that the officer's job I was paid to do, and tried to do, seldom left time for more than the matter at hand. Whenever I heard about folks' lives outside the union context, I realized how narrow a view I had. According to Mrs. Rowan, Nick went out every Wednesday night for church choir.

"Well, isn't that grand!" I chuckled. I hadn't meant to sound so phony, but I think Mrs. Rowan took it in the right spirit. She told me Nick had left a message for me and went to get it.

"Mr. Morrow? Nick said the ship departed without us loading the gear. And then he said the boxes were shifted or left on the dock."

"Thank you. Could you tell Nick I'll call him tomorrow at work?"

"The minute he's home."

We said our goodbyes and hung up. I thought about how I never get the chance to catch up with Nick, or anyone else. I went to what I called my 'medicine chest' and refreshed my drink. I knew Michael McSweeney, the terminal boss I'd crossed swords with earlier, would be up, so I decided to give him a call and get him real riled up.

He still sounded sour as he picked up the phone.

"Hello?"

"McSweeney! You still sound like you need that snooze and a horn or two."

"Very funny, Morrow. I'm dying of laughter, here." He went on to say that with the specs and snaps in hand, he had something in mind.

I asked what he meant and he said it was something to talk over. Now, I knew he'd try to get my okay for whatever he had planned *before* seeing the final results, because making changes to whatever he had readied would also entail significant cost. But he was on the back foot here. The only reason he wouldn't tell the dayside crew to work that faulty lashing is if he knew he'd stand no chance in an arbitration. So I wasn't having any of it.

"Start with sketches and move to plans and draft your diagrams because you need to specify in black and white how to make things safe. Only when you've done that can you start your prefab work."

McSweeney replied, "But even before we do any sketching, we'd like you to be here. We'd want your input."

"Look, I've already said that I'll be really lucky to make it at all, anytime, tomorrow. I was still thinking of trying for 10:00, but now I'll tell you this: I'm not going to use what time I have hearing the things you've 'got in mind.' If I'm coming over, I want to see things on paper."

"Say we had our paperwork by 10:00 tomorrow morning. You'd come over to take a look and have a talk?"

"Yeah, if you have things down on paper by then, I'm willing to try to be there."

"We'll get started by midnight or so," McSweeney said, "and I'll call you at eight in the morning to confirm that you will show up at ten."

"Okay, that sounds good." McSweeney said thanks for the call, and I had to smile.

It was just after eight by then, and I had to make a call—one I was real sorry to have to make—to a lady friend, to cancel a date for supper and a movie on this coming Saturday. We had talked, too, about driving the next day to Point Reyes. In fact, we had been talking a lot over the past couple of months and, because she was union, too, I had only to mention the aid and touch on the *Star*, and she was on board. We were both sorry and said so. But she understood.

"Because this is hush-hush, I don't need to hear more," she said. "So just keep the faith—and good for you, and everyone else. Call me when you can."

I hung up, microwaved some leftover lasagna, and waited to hear from Tom. After a few minutes of radio silence, my eyes grew heavier, and I dozed off in nothing flat.

The phone woke me with a start. I had no idea how long I'd been out for, but the tone in Tom's voice told me I better wake up fast.

"Steve, I have terrible news."

"What's doing?"

"We learned at 6:00 this evening that four American religious women are missing in El Salvador."

"Oh my god."

"We got the news at quarter to six from the Maryknoll center in Ossining, New York, which I ought to say will be our main source on this. An Ursuline sister, Dorothy Kazel, and a lay volunteer, Ms. Jean Donovan, who are stationed at a Cleveland-sponsored mission in the coastal city La Libertad, drove to the airport to meet two Maryknollers, Ita Ford and Maura Clarke. They were expected back by seven, but when at midnight they had still not arrived, the mission called the civil authorities, U.S. Embassy, Cleveland Archdiocese, and the center in Ossining.

"Ambassador White has really been good, but the junta and some of the Washington folks, maybe to get their cover in place, have been stalling and stonewalling. When little, if anything, had been done by five o'clock this morning, White was raising Cain with the State Department, but even then, it took until noon, San Salvador time, to get them listed as missing. And it took two more hours to mount, in theory, at least, a so-called search, which was called off at five, to be resumed later in the morning. We met then with the Archdiocesan staff, but now we can only wait."

"Yeah," I said. "I understand."

"You'll be in your office by six? If you can, give me a call first thing."

The call shook me to my core. Normally before I hit the hay, I always made a list of what I'd have to do the next day, but today I was too anxious. Instead, I finished my drink as I stared out into the stormy night. Vowing to do everything in my power to defeat the vicious fascist junta, I got to bed and fell into a fitful sleep, filled with bad dreams.

13

"Have you seen today's *Chronicle*?"

It was shortly after five, the sun was still in the ground, and I hadn't even seen a cup of joe yet. Tom Augustine, who was on the other end of the phone, informed me there was an article confirming the disappearance of the Maryknollers.

"There's more Steve. And it's worse. About an hour after we spoke last night, I got a call from Ossining. The van the women were driving. It's been found–burned."

"Oh God." My heart sank. But my determination to stop the arms shipment hardened all the more. I thought, *screw the PCMA, screw the contract, screw the government, we can't send these monsters one single solitary bullet.*

Tom and I agreed to stay in touch and hung up. I threw on my black Frisco jeans and a Hickory shirt, then hit the road. Another day that promised rain. Another day on the job.

I stopped at a corner to pick up a coffee and a *Chron.* There wasn't much on the women. Where they'd been, where they'd been going, and how and when the van was found. Then the article shifted to the funeral of the folks supposedly killed by the revolutionary democratic front.

I arrived in my office at ten to six, switched on the overhead fluorescents, put my briefcase on the desk, and set about my morning chores– revving up the copy machine, opening the walk-in safe, checking the mail, and most importantly, brewing a pot of strong coffee.

When I got back to my desk I found a visitor waiting for me. Brother Russ Taylor, an old pal. He smiled and laid out a neatly folded newspaper piece on my desk. Before even unfolding it I knew it would be about asbestos. Russ had worked with a guy, Max, who in 1975 had died due to asbestosis. They'd been partners for thirty-three years–first in the hold, then on the winches, and, finally, under the hook on the dock. Back then none of us knew the dangers of the stuff. But when Max got diagnosed, the two of them set about educating the workers. Before long, we were all refusing to work with it or even be around it. When Max died, it became Russ's cause.

This article was about a docker down in LA who filed for state workmen's comp when he was told that he had "white lung." Although he since died, the claim had just been sustained by a hearing board.

"It'll be appealed of course, but this could be a big step to a guy at least getting *something* while they're waiting to die," Russ said.

"Right." I smiled, feeling some hope at the prospect of compensating workers for an illness caused by work conditions.

When Russ went off to make some copies of the article, I opened my mail. I had a letter from the Committee to Save Kim Dae-jung. Tom's clergy group had turned me onto some of the troubling political events in the Republic of Korea and I always wanted to stay abreast. In 1971, massive governmental fraud had denied Kim the presidency. In 1980 he was convicted on trumped up charges of treason and sedition and sentenced to death by hanging. It was ridiculous and undoubtably connected with larger global injustices related to Reagan's cold war campaign.

The mailer predicted that Kim's sentence would be carried out within a few weeks, then proposed: OUR ONLY RECOURSE: WIRES OF APPEAL TO CHUN DOO-HWAN FOR CLEMENCY.

I thought about what we could do. If we refused to load the arms for the junta prior to Kim's hanging, then at the time of our refusal, we could also announce that if Kim was executed we would no longer work any ships from the Republic of Korea.

Just as I finished my mail, several men flooded into my office. They were from that walkout over the absent carbon monoxide testing meter on Pier 27, and they were here to file a claim. Fred Darwin, the steward for 27, gave me the jive. Apparently, the company rep who accused the workers of stealing his meter had had a flat tire that morning. This rep always kept his meter case in the car. When he got the flat, the company motor pool took the car in to have its tire changed and gave the rep another car to take to work. Long story short, he forgot to take his meter case before he drove away in his replacement car.

Fred's brother Simon just happened to work in the motor pool, so Fred called him up. Simon got a company Polaroid, propped the front page of that day's *Examiner* against the "stolen" case, and took some snaps. Simon joked, "If the rep saw these in private, we could save money and time by getting a confession of blackmail."

We all had a big laugh over what Fred called "The Case of the Missing Meter Case."

14

A couple minutes after I'd finished filing their claims, the beeper on my belt went off. It was my union president, Paul Murphy. The guys all cleared out and I called in to Paul. He said there was no news on the missing Maryknoll women, and we agreed to hold off on discussing the refusal to load arms until they were found. Or until we found out they weren't going to be found.

"In the meantime, why don't you contact your guy over at the *Chronicle*?"

Jim Birch was a reporter I knew over at the *San Francisco Chronicle-Examiner*. He was always my go-to when I had a headline scoop.

"Sure thing."

"Thanks. Now," Paul went on, "while we're waiting for news, can we talk about Kim?"

Apparently, Paul was also on the Worldwide Committee to Save Kim Dae-jung mailing list. He said, "They're saying maybe three weeks max before he gets hanged. They're also asking folks to wire an appeal for clemency to General Chun. And I was thinking– maybe we could 'piggyback' his fate to our refusal to handle the junta aid."

"How do you mean 'piggyback'?" I asked.

"I've not thought this through, so my answer might be scrambled. But whatever date the execution's set for, we need to send our clemency plea before then, right? So we could say in our plea that if they hang Kim, we'll take appropriate action. I don't have the wording fully in mind, but make it clear that we'll do something."

After a moment I realized I'd been nodding my head at the phone instead of saying anything.

"In other words, our appeal for clemency would include a threat."

"Exactly. Now, hold that point. The Korean CIA has informers and agents in every Korean community in the United States. You know that, right?" I said I did. "So, we can assume that every pro-Kim committee has been infiltrated."

"That seems safe to assume."

"So, say a few days before Kim's execution, one or two agents just *happen* to learn that if they hang Kim, we'll refuse to work any South Korean ships. I'm just wondering how we'd make sure the agents got that information."

"I could meet with the students, swearing them to secrecy, trusting that some agents were among them."

"Hm, interesting. But what if they leak it to the press or the FBI?"

"What damage could that do? If the FBI came to us about rumors of a planned retaliation, we'd say someone was making up fairy tales."

"I don't know. It sounds good, but I don't want to do anything rash without thinking of all the potential consequences. Let's mull it over and talk again soon."

I agreed and we hung up. I quickly dropped a line to Jim. The *Examiner's* number–777-7777–was never too tricky to remember. He quickly agreed to meet in the afternoon.

15

There are very few guarantees in life. So in a way it was reassuring that whatever day it was, I'd get a phone call from terminal boss Michael McSweeney with his regular jive.

"Listen Morrow, I'm just calling to make sure you show up to this thing at ten." McSweeney had a raspy voice, probably from all the cigarettes he inhaled. Maybe from too much whiskey, too.

"Oh don't you worry, I'll be there. But just so you know, I can't stay past two o'clock today and I'm booked up tomorrow."

"With all the bigwigs showing up, I think we'll finish no later than noon."

"Good, but what the hell have you got in mind? It sounds like a summit or something."

"We want this problem solved. And I was just thinking that we—I mean you, me and your gear shop boss—might get together for a little chat."

"Oh, for Christ's sake. We've already lost a shit pot full of boxes. And we're talking about refitting six ships here. Do you seriously expect me to believe it's just a 'little' chat? What bigwigs are coming to this shindig, anyhow?"

"Some of my people—my boss from LA—and, naturally, the steamship side."

I faked a glum voice.

"So, how many people?"

"I don't know. Maybe a dozen or so."

"And will they all have something to say, or what?"

"Hey, listen. They'll talk more than we do."

"That's my goddamned point. I mean, they can talk all they want, but I've got to leave by two."

"Don't worry, we'll be long gone by one," McSweeney said.

"Well, okay, see you at ten," and I hung up.

The truth was, I was happy all the bigwigs would show. It meant I'd be able to screw them all in one fell swoop. Still, I needed an excuse to bail out of McSweeney's meeting if they tried to hold me there, and I had just the thing.

Word had gotten around recently that our union had begun a campaign to bring all the machines for moving freight up to our safety code. The day before, John Tilby, dock steward at Pier 32, had called because some lifts on his dock needed "major maintenance and minor repairs." We had agreed that, after briefing the drivers, we'd begin at the morning coffee break to have them stop work and stand by until their machines were up to code. To that end, John agreed to prepare the key information: a list of what each lift needed. And right after my call with McSweeney, John got back to me.

"Some of the lifts have pretty bad brakes and some have no horns. Some have hydraulic leaks, others, smoky exhausts. Oil has dripped from pans, engine blocks are loaded with crud, some of the steering gear is bad, and some forklifts can hardly move. Some are just a menace."

"Jesus, what *isn't* wrong? How many are there?"

"How many in all?"

"Lifts or beefs?"

"Lifts."

"A total of eight."

"You gotta be kidding me. This was a made-to-order opportunity to put one over on the terminal boss.

"Okay. I've got my own beef with old McSweeney on Seventh Street. I'll tell you about it when I see you. But we've got to coordinate."

"Sure."

"I'm meeting with him at ten. And I want to get out of there no later than eleven. In other words, I want to meet him, but only to draw him out. Have you got that?"

"Yeah, I got it."

"Good. Now, you've got to set up some calls about the lifts and stopping work. You should start calling at coffee time and continue for an hour or so. Once I've found out from McSweeney what I want to know, I want him to understand that I have to leave because of those calls. I'm going to ask our answering service to put all my calls to *his* office."

"So I call you at McSweeney's office to tell you we'll be stopping work."

"Exactly. But that's not the end of it. After you call me, at ten-thirty or so, I want you to go back and tell *your* pier boss Webster that I'm being tied up by McSweeney, and that *he* should call McSweeney to complain. I want Webster to rattle *his* boss's cage for tying me up when he's facing a work stoppage—one that involves a vessel on berth."

John chuckled. "That'll work."

Guys like John Tilby are key to getting the work done.

Back to thinking about McSweeney. Given all the wigs coming to the summit, there'd be a real effort to nail me down by Friday morn. Tilby's calls would get me out of the meeting, but I needed something more lasting. What I needed was a one-two punch that would make them back off until the end of the following day. I had a good idea of what might work.

I called Al Richards, the steward at Pier 15. Al had told me he was dealing with excessive engine noise from the lifts. The lifts were scheduled to have their mechanical bridles refitted with vacuum-powered ones. It speeds up handling and reduces damage. There's just one problem: the vacuum required a small gas engine mounted right behind the lift driver's seat that made a hellish noise. When the pier boss couldn't find his fricking noise meter, he (Al) had tested the first six lifts that were refitted himself. Sure enough, he was right, the noise was way above what our safety code permitted, and what OSHA said we had to live with.

Al ended with: "My supervisor Joe Monteith just wants the shipping company to make their dough at our expense."

I told Al that Monteith *had* to test the noise level of each lift according to OSHA's safety code, *and* our own. If the noise was low enough, the drivers would work a full shift. But if the noise level over a full eight hours would be too high, we'd shut down the lifts and send the drivers home— with pay for eight hours. Al agreed to call McSweeney's office around ten-thirty, saying I was needed right away at Pier 15.

"That ought to slow them down a bit," I told him.

"Yeah, right. Good plan, Steve."

16

It was then ten to eight in the morning. I heard another buzz; Anthony Alvarez, from an ILWU local up the west coast, was on the line. He wanted to get the skinny on the aid shipments and see where we were at.

Anthony asked, "You've seen the latest news about the four missing American nuns in El Salvador?"

"Sure have," I replied.

"Assuming the worst, which I always do, we've got to watch out for the down-home bigotry. This kind of thing could really help the Reaganites. Which actually gets me to my other reason for calling. Our local's internal problems."

Let me give some background. We had a cannery local that dispatched a lot of folks to Alaska from its hall. In early 1979 a gang of crooks began to infiltrate that stream of workers. They began with dice and cards and horse and dog races, often underwritten by heavy loan-sharking. And some said that, for reasons of "morale," ladies of dubious character were being dispatched to Alaska, too.

As the gang gained more influence in the union, opposition arose. Many of the Local's ranks were Filipino, who generally supported Reagan's cold war foreign policy. As the local's election approached, the gang decided to say they also supported Reagan and Marcos to win votes. One of the gang leaders had won secretary-treasurer and a second was elected dispatcher. Now Alvarez brought me up-to-date.

"Since the election, things have gotten uglier. Some guys are calling for honest elections in the local, and the gangsters aren't liking that. A half dozen brawls have broken out in and around the hall."

"That's rough, brother. What can I do?"

"The brothers calling for honest elections will be coming to San Fran today so they can meet with President Murphy and his crew tomorrow morning. I know with the whole Salvadoran situation this is a bad time for you. But I told them to go see you and Frank because they'd like some friends at our national convention in April. I mean, it's being rumored now that, literally as we convene, Marcos will be an honored guest at the Reagan White House. I want you to know that these are really good union guys, caught up in a hell of a battle. So if they show up, I hope you'll do what you can."

"Of course. What are their names?"

"Montebon. Margarito Montebon. He's the secretary. He's twenty-nine, with a wife and two kids. And Gus Vincenti. He's single and also twenty-nine. They're staying on Lombard Street. Maybe take them to Sabella's for supper?"

"That sounds great. Thanks for the straight dope, Anthony. And take care."

Next, I wanted to follow up on the brother who suffered a fall and got hurt. I called the boss and the steward of the gang the brother had been working with to get their views on how he had fallen. They both ruled it an accident, which means that neither the ship nor the stevedore firm could be deemed at fault. They said he was where he was supposed to be, doing what he was supposed to be doing for working coils of steel in a wing.

I asked what I always asked: how long was the wait for an ambulance? Since it had taken some time for the brother to be moved from the wing to the dock, the ambulance already was waiting for him. Both of them confirmed that an accident report had been filed with the stevedore. I signed off by noting that the brother was a "really good guy" who had caught a "tough break." I thanked them for the good work they had done and said I'd call the injured brother now.

His daughter answered the phone. She said her dad was in a lot of pain after a fitful night. I got him on the line and told him if there was anything I could do for him to let me know. All he said was: "Just another accident. But here's my daughter, again."

She thanked me and I clumsily signed off. Those were always the toughest calls to make. I took a folder of info for Margarito and Gus and headed over to Frank Spaulding's office in Local 10.

I'm real proud of Local 10's building and grounds. It's been our home since the late fifties. This is where business gets taken care of. With its manicured grounds and distinctive rotunda, the complex has been widely acclaimed "a notable addition to the city's architecture." It does justice to the work that's done inside its walls.

Frank Spaulding had what are called ruggedly chiseled good looks– a cliché, but true. His deeply lined face was partly due to his sixty-plus years of life, but mostly because in that time he had attended the school of hard knocks. He had a well-knit frame, broad shoulders and stood an inch or two over six feet. His hair was a thick, unruly, wavy black mane, graying at the temples, and his hands were large and knobby.

As for his character, he once told me (when half in the bag): "With all the mouths to feed and the Brooklyn waterfront not a block away, at fourteen I up and left me old mother dear, bless her soul, and went to sea." Having thus launched, he'd gone on at age seventeen to fight in the Spanish Civil War, where he was wounded. After that, he fought in World War II, sailing the Murmansk run. Back in San Francisco after the war, he worked and struggled in and for the National Maritime Union until Joe McCarthy spread his cold war poison, and Frank lost his right to have a berth. Screened out of work at sea, he ended up in Local 10.

In spite of his hard times, Frank had a good sense of humor and was always looking to enjoy himself. It was said that he'd spent time with women of every view and outlook, and some with neither. I always thought of him as a left-wing Marlboro man. And he was more than ready to handle the challenges of a shipment south.

"Well, what have you got for my welcome home?" he said as I entered his office, putting the paper to one side.

"You'll know soon enough." I took a chair and caught him up on everything I knew about the junta aid. He had heard drips and drabs and had read about the nuns, but still, he was stunned. When I finished, he leafed through his papers, shook his head, and said: "The winds of this war are freshening. The lousy bastards."

We talked for a while about the South Korean situation too, then got onto the anti-Marcos stuff. Frank told me Mahoney had called him, too. He suggested dinner "at Sabella's about six."

"That would be great, but I'll have to call you later on."

I checked my watch. It was nine fifteen, so I had to roll.

"Frank, do me a favor. If McSweeney calls, tell him I'm at Pier 32 with the lift drivers standing by."

Frank nodded, saying, "I don't have the faintest idea about any of that, but if that's what you want me to say, that's what he'll get."

17

McSweeney's office was all the way out in Oakland. I usually hit the trail early because traffic frequently backed up on the Bay Bridge. I was irritated by a crack he made once that I was always late. Today the roads were clear, so I got there in record time, giving him a nice surprise when I was there early. Then right as the meeting was about to begin, I decided to go to the can so it'd start late anyway.

There were a lot of heavy hitters in the conference room. McSweeney 's boss, two people from the steamship line, two design folks from an Oakland yard, two from its prefab shop, his safety director, his gear locker boss, and his maintenance boss. I passed around a sign-in sheet to get all the names. Meanwhile, McSweeney described his bench and paperwork with a wide expanse.

"Let's be out of here by noon. I guess Morrow, who's on time for a change, is fine with that. I mean, since you were actually early, it must be really slow on the front."

I thought of a couple things I could have said but decided to just smile.

"I'm all for moving along."

McSweeney handed out his elaborate paperwork and explained:

"As you see here, I've got a dozen stacks of documents. Snaps of each ladder, each pedestal, each platform, taken at every conceivable angle. Above and beyond. We also have sketches of the ship's catwalk, and if needed, several copies of the blueprints."

Unsurprisingly, I was the only one who actually looked at the snaps. Everyone on the boss's side was waiting for me—and that was fine and dandy, as far as I was concerned. Right as I started to make some comments, his secretary came in. She said she had a message for me. The timing was great. I read the note aloud:

"Pier 32 Local 10 Steward. Drivers will stop work at one over faulty, unsafe lift machines." Then I casually set it aside, fighting the urge to laugh.

"You know what, McSweeney, these forward frame sketches are darned good."

In a few minutes, the secretary returned with another note.

"Two more calls from 32."

Ten minutes later, another note, this time from Pier 15: "Work to stop at 1 P.M. due to excessive noise from vacuum lifts."

At this point the guys were all getting pretty curious. Before I could even thank the secretary, she turned to her boss and said there was an urgent call for him from a pier supervisor Jack Webster at Pier 32.

I felt myself starting to laugh again, and had to fake a cough to cover it up. McSweeney left to take the call and I ploughed ahead with some more of my serious talk about the ship. Then I set things into motion.

"I'd love to talk more about the master sketch of the aft catwalk, gentlemen. But take a look at this."

I passed around my big stack of notes, then continued: "We're running shorthanded today, so it's starting to look bad for me. But who knows? Maybe these things will just go away."

"How do you mean, just go away?" one of the bigwigs asked.

"You probably know that lousy lifts are not exactly hard to find, so it could be that a driver or two or even more aren't happy, but at the same time they are saying only that they ought to stop work after lunch."

"So the call for stoppage might fizzle out?"

"Could do. Then again, anything to do with lifts can really mushroom out of nowhere, spread like a prairie fire. But don't worry. If I have to leave, you guys can all hang around here and I'll try to get back."

At that everyone in the room exploded.

"Someone running some other pier shouldn't be allowed to cut in line! We've already lost a whole lot of dough, and now we're being made to wait in line just to be allowed to spend more!"

"I know. But you already know, or at least you should, that a work stoppage always cuts to the front of the line. *You* guys made that rule, not me. And with all the smarts on your team, this should be a real cakewalk for you."

The heads all grumbled at each other while I tried to redirect their attention to the prefabbed frame renderings on page nine.

Right then McSweeney's gal Friday came back through the door and held up another note. For the kick of it, I asked her to read it to me this time.

"Message from Local 10: work stoppage to start at 1 p.m. at Pier 32 due to faulty, unsafe lift machines."

I checked my watch. 10:45. Damn, if we're not right on schedule.

McSweeney came bumbling back into the room.

"This I can't believe, but Webster is saying that come one o'clock, a dozen lift drivers will stop and stand by. Some bullshit about faulty lifts and a little noise problem."

I passed him my notes and, when his butt was mere inches away from his chair, the secretary opened the door again.

"Urgent call, sir. From the supervisor at Pier 15. He wants to know what to do about the work stoppage."

Her boss's face froze. "Well I'll be a son of a bitch."

I wish I'd had my camera right then.

We continued to review the documents while he was gone. He came back looking severely stressed.

"Can you fucking believe this! Now some jagoff down at Pier 15 is saying that a dozen lifts need to be tested for noise or *they're* gonna stop at one, too!"

I raised both my hands apologetically.

"Sorry fellas. If you want to wait around here I'll try come back. But no guarantees. Who knows how long this could take."

And with that I was gone. I'd snookered them pretty well.

18

It was almost eleven thirty when John Tilby and I spotted each other out front of Pier 32. I smiled as the resourceful steward filled me in. The pier supervisor had decided to keep the lifts on the dock because, if they were used on the ship, stopping them would be a lot more disruptive.

"He's waiting to hear from you," Tilby continued. "But after that you can buy lunch for me and the guys at the Java House." He laughed and started punching the air, getting ready for the fight.

Pier Superintendent Jack Webster was a dead ringer for Al Capone. When I came in, he didn't say diddly-squat. He just wore a stern and sour face and gave me a begrudging nod. I met his stern gaze and told him he'd be well advised to just get the eight good lifts he'd need.

"But you've not even seen the lifts!" Webster burst out.

"Hey, the contract says nothing about my duty to look. If you want to raise that issue, just get to the end of the line. I'm not going to look at any of your lifts. And that's because, first, I don't second-guess a steward like brother Tilby. And second, if we go that route, we will all be looking at every machine."

He grumbled but didn't contradict me.

Right then his phone rang, and I heard exactly what I wanted to: "It's for you. Local Ten."

Shirley asked me if Webster had told me about her earlier call about the issue at Pier 15. I scowled at him.

"No, he never mentioned it. I said I hoped to be back at McSweeney's by three."

"Sounds like a typical day."

I hung up and stared at Webster. "You know I'm supposed to go down to Pier 15 about a noise abatement problem with the lifts, there, right"

"Not my problem," he said. "Look Morrow. You know we have only a single rig for hauling lifts around."

"So?"

"Well, it can haul only four at a time, so you're talking about making two trips."

"You can do whatever you want. I hope you wise up and play things straight, and I'll be back as soon as I can."

"But I'm not sure I can get eight lifts."

I just shrugged, letting him sweat. I had him right where I wanted him.

The phone rang again. Webster slowly picked it up.

"Pier Thirty-two," he sighed, then handed me the phone.

"Al? How'd you know I was here? Oh! Well Shirley, she's just dynamite. As she said, thirty-two was first in line, but I'll be right at your place no later than one. Yes, even if they *stop work* here."

Before I'd even hung up, Webster was on another phone ordering eight new lifts.

Before leaving, I decided to play the bosses against each other a little, see if I couldn't turn two problems into each other's solution.

"Good decision, Webster. I want to get your guys back to work on these new lifts. But you guys know how McSweeney's on my ass. To make sure he doesn't cut in line, if he calls just tell him the situation is the same as it was."

"Of course. Just make sure this gets settled."

And with that I was out of there.

I went down to the Java House and gave John and the guys the good news: in an hour or so, they'd be getting other lifts. They were all over the moon, clapping and smiling and raising their coffees and sodas to the sky. They asked me to stay for a hot dog and join in the celebration, but unfortunately, I had to refuse, there was still work to be done.

I met Al Richards over at Pier 15. The two of us marched up to the office of Superintendent Joe Montieth, a heavyset fella with hair on every part of his body except his head. He'd gotten the job running the paper dock when a local bigshot in the newsprint game married a daughter of his. Figures.

"Mister Morrow, qué pasó?"

"Jo-Jo, how are you?"

He raised his ham hock arms into a shrug.

"Ponies no good. Market no good. But I know you don't play those games."

"I can't afford to gamble."

"The way I'm losing money, I'd kill to be as broke as you."

We had a nice chuckle. Monteith went on: "So, what are we talkin' about today?"

"Your vacuum lifts. They're way too noisy." His cheery face sobered.

"They are brand new and cost big dough."

Once again, the phone rang. My game was running like clockwork, and I couldn't help but feel a little pride.

"McSweeney? Yeah, Morrow's here. Why you asking?"

I could hear McSweeney's voice raised on the other end of the line, and Montieth scowled back into the receiver.

"Now you listen here, McSweeney! Morrow and I have a big matter to discuss, and you don't butt in here any time you feel like!"

While McSweeney did some more yelling, Montieth cupped the phone to his chest and rolled his eyes.

"That fucking mick, damned son of an Irish whore."

Joe passed me the phone. McSweeney yelled in my ear: "Morrow! You know I won't be able to get squat done unless you're here. You're tying me up with ten goddamn people while you drive all over town."

I tried to sound as innocent as possible.

"Hey, wait a minute now, my friend. You've only got to do the right thing, and you've got ten people to help you."

"But, look," he protested. "They're not gonna spend anything like this kind of dough."

"Oh, for Christ's sake. Tell them I work for the men. Not the other way around."

McSweeney sighed.

"We'll be waiting for you, okay? Just show up as soon as possible."

I hung up and returned to Montieth, who said, "Let's cut to the chase, Morrow. What do you want?"

"We need the noise testing OSHA calls for. Tomorrow would be good."

"How do I do it tomorrow?"

"Do it *Monday* if you like. Or *Tuesday*. Take as long as would please you. But nobody will be working those vacuum lifts until it's been done."

"Fine, fine. Tomorrow."

"Great. Call who you need to call, then confirm it with me over at McSweeney's."

"And I'll call the son of a bitch who suggested to modify the lifts instead of buying new ones."

"Right, because it was *his* job to read the OSHA regulations. *And* the union rules." I couldn't help myself.

After that it was another spin over to Pier 32. This time supervisor Webster greeted me with big smiles, wanting to keep everything copacetic. Heck, the boss even offered me his desk! I told them that I wanted to call McSweeney to stop him from thinking of some way to cut in line.

McSweeney answered the phone sounding relieved and surprisingly bouncy.

"Morrow! I knew you'd call. I told the guys for sure you'd be back today. The coffee's on, and I got you a lunch, so we're ready to roll."

"Oof. Listen, McSweeney. I'm sitting with Webster now at pier 32, and we just this moment signed off on what gets fixed on the lifts we've got." I winked at Webster. "But given the time and the lifts that still have to be checked, I just can't say I'll get back. And for tomorrow I also have a big noise test on Pier 15 that will take most of the day."

The bounce drained from McSweeney's voice as he realized I was peeing on his parade. It felt like he had a million things he wanted to say to me, but all he could get out was: "Just be in touch."

19

The Treasure Chest, our only gin mill left from the good old days, was a favorite for me and lots of other guys. Because it was closer to Pier Thirty-two than even the paper dock at Fifteen, I could be back in nothing flat if I got a beep. I got a black coffee and a dollar's worth of dimes and sat myself next to the pay phone. I took a couple of sips, checked my watch, then dialed Tom Augustine.

Tom reported that the search for the Maryknoll Sisters was continuing and Washington was up-in-arms, but there were no updates on the safety and rescue front. He also said that Maria Martinez wanted to meet with us as soon as possible. Maria was a refugee who lost a husband and a son in El Salvador. I had heard her speak at community events and had great respect for her and her work. She led a group helping fellow refugees who had long been a target of the junta's goons and spies.

"Sure. Any time, any place."

"She sees her staff at six. How about five?"

"Yeah, sure. But why does she want to meet?"

"She's always guarded on the phone, but as part of her refugee work, she's been tracking the climate in the Mission District. She can fill us in on local security matters."

I heard a voice in the background of Tom's line.

"Steve, I'm getting another call. I've got to take it, it could be related to the search."

"Sure thing, friend."

I went back to my coffee and looked over John's paperwork. I started eyeing some pudding over on the counter–the house specialty–when my beeper went off. It was Tom again already. And it was urgent.

I dialed immediately.

"Tom?"

"Steve, there's no easy way to say this. All the women, they've been…they've been killed."

My breath caught against my throat and I had to lean against the wall. I had gotten so sucked into the other fights of the day, I really wasn't expecting this blow when it came. Tom's voice stayed clinical as he tried to give me the information, but underneath it I could tell he was shaken.

"I got the call from the Maryknollers right after we hung up. The four women were found in a shallow common grave by a country road. All of them shot in the back of the head. Molested, and possibly raped. The *Examiner* is squeezing it in on page three."

"Damn."

"I know. And at a memorial mass for them today, a peasant was killed."

I tried to keep a level head. "How's the response been?"

"Ambassador White has been terrific. He's really raised hell with the junta because a Canadian religious group were stopped and threatened by junta troops near the exact same spot. Of course, nobody's writing about that."

Tom continued: "Back here, Maria's refugee group are sponsoring a gathering of remembrance, tomorrow at eight at the Mission San Francisco de Asis. Do you know it?"

I told Tom I'd driven by the beautiful church but had never been inside.

"Well, it will be packed tomorrow night. Maria is inviting those from the stream of refugees as honored guests. We'll remember Romero and call out his name, and those at the gathering will call out *'Presente!'* for El Salvador's recent martyrs, the FDR folks, and finally, the sisters."

"And what about today?"

"Well, Maria and I still want to meet."

We signed off. I dropped another dime in the phone. Paul Murphy–no surprise–had already heard the news from our D.C. rep, a docker named Mike Garvey. According to Garvey, the women had been raped. That information was later confirmed by the press and, eventually, the U.S. government. But we got it first from Mike.

20

Frank had delayed printing the union bulletin because he thought an update might come in. Now he frantically scribbled at the other end of the phone while I read off what Tom and Paul had said. Shirley and Dolores Rodriquez, the other office mainstay at Local 10, had agreed to stay late if that's what it took to get the news out on time.

"Also, Steve, I don't know if now is the right time, but Margarito Montebon called. He and Gus will be here at four, but they need to leave at six to get up to their meeting in Oakland."

"Shoot. That's no good for me. Tell them I'm sorry, and I'll try my damnedest to see them tomorrow."

"Sure thing, but they'll understand if you're tied up."

I was almost out the door when my phone rang. *Damn. No rest for the weary.* It was Doug Martin, confirming that yes, the *Star* would be in port sometime after midnight Friday and ready to load from Pier 50 early Saturday morning. I thanked Doug and headed over for my meeting with my reporter friend Jim Birch. We met at a near-empty Chinese restaurant on Howard because we wanted some privacy and Jim had been "too busy chasing a wild goose to eat."

We exchanged pleasantries and ordered, then Jim spotted the folder in my hand with his name on it. His eyes lit up behind his horn-rimmed glasses. He reminded me a lot of Clark Kent.

"What have you got there?"

I handed him the document.

"Based on the smile on your face, I can tell you haven't seen your three-p.m. edition."

Glancing at my clipping, his face fell.

"Jesus."

"Anyway, that's not what I'm here for. Take a gander at what we've got now down on 50-D."

While he looked over the pics of the arms shipment in Shed D, I went to make a quick call to Minister John Boyer. I was hoping to set up a meeting with him and Tom Augustine to talk about Kim and Korea. Talk about luck–John and Reverend Roger Morris were planning to have a meeting at six about the church campaign to try and stop the execution of former President Kim!

The waitress followed me back to the booth with our orders in hand. We thanked her and started right in. Jim shoveled in his Hunan beef without looking up, engrossed as he was by the snaps.

When he finally finished his meal and his reading, I explained the whole thing from my perspective. I took special care to outline how the aid could be crucial to a new junta offensive, as I knew this information would be crucial to gaining public support from the article. Finally, I laid out our plan to announce the wildcat stoppage "on the individual moral stance of each and every docker," and that the whole shebang might kick off this Saturday, if they try to load the arms on the *Star*. There was his scoop.

Jim was completely bowled over with the whole tale, and he seemed excited to tell our story. When I added that Maria Martinez was organizing a memorial service for the four slain Maryknoller sisters, as well as the many civilians murdered by the death squads, he promised to cover it, too.

Jim insisted on paying the check ("and I'll hear no more about it!") and I got my coat. He said he was going to hang a while to review the notes he'd made, so I left him to it.

Still no traffic in the grey city streets. Still, the hanging promise of rain.

21

Maria Martinez was a small, almost frail woman in her late forties. Her thin face emphasized strong features and a piercing set of black eyes. A silver brooch shimmered off her gray pinstripe suit. An air of sorrow hung around her, but she punched through it with a sense of ready determination. We shook hands as Tom introduced us.

"It's a shame you have to meet under such circumstances," he said as we each took a seat in his office, "but given the prospect of the union's refusal to load aid, I felt it was important. My feeling at the moment is that if the union refuses to handle the aid, the local junta forces will escalate their violence."

He then gestured to Maria, who told me the following story:

"There is a growing level of violence being used against our forces for change here in America. This violence is the direct result of the work of Guillermo Hernandez."

She explained that Guillermo Hernandez, the eldest brother of Colonel Tomás Hernandez, was the named recipient of the U.S. military aid. The Hernandezes were a wealthy, powerful family with a rich history of right-wing politics. Their grandfather, General M Hernandez, crushed a peasant revolt in 1931, and subsequently the most fearsome death squad in the country was named after him.

As the family multiplied and expanded, they took more and more power in El Salvador. One brother managed the family lands, which held vast expanses of coffee, cotton and cattle farms. Another was an assistant to the minister of justice who locked up people or had them shot. A third was a priest who ignored the poor and served the rich.

Guillermo Hernandez arrived in San Francisco in 1979 claiming to be a refugee from the bloodless coup. He set up shop at a swanky hotel, and over the next three months, he ensconced himself in the Reagan camp. Eventually he moved to the consulate to become part of Reagan's campaign. Hernandez and the consul-general set to work preaching panic about "the communist terror of the Central American forces run by Russia," presenting themselves as freedom fighters.

Guillermo funded and spoke on behalf of an organization called the United Salvadoran Patriotic Forces, or FUPS (an acronym of its Spanish name). FUPS was an overtly pro-junta and anti-communist group, with offices in both Los Angeles and San Francisco. Maria said the organization was still small in San Fran, but it caused a lot of fear among Salvadoran refugees and the larger immigrant community. In its so-called "community work" the FUPS were approaching Salvadoran immigrants and pressuring them into declaring vocal support for the FUPS's cause. Despite their size, they'd created a disciplined network of informers, agents, spies, and thugs, with friends in the INS.

FUPS set up a cadre of about a dozen members designed to track and threaten anti-junta folks in the Bay Area. Recently those threats had increased. Threatening calls were placed frequently. A rotation of squads had begun to park overnight in front of the homes of Maria's colleagues. Even more terrifying, someone in the INS appeared to have given FUPS the files of a number of folks seeking asylum from El Salvador.

In response, Maria set up neighborhood watches with phone trees. The most at-risk people were moved around, with security, in car caravans. These drivers had been trained in defensive measures to escape pursuers and break up car caravans for safety.

But in the last couple of weeks the violence had escalated severely. Before, they had pushed, shoved, torn away protesters' signs. Now they were using fists. All this came to a head the preceding Monday at UC Berkeley, where the FUPS rushed a demonstration protesting the FDR killings and attacked those participating.

In concluding, Maria said when she heard about the union's potential action, she wanted to warn us immediately about the FUPS threat. "Be careful, Steve. Be *very* careful, and try not to travel alone. Especially at night."

I told her I was staggered by her story and would exercise caution. We all agreed to warn anyone and everyone we tried to involve.

The talk then turned to the four murdered women. Tom told us about an outlandish statement made by the head of the junta, José Napoléon Duarte, claiming that the murders were carried out by insurrectionist groups "to destabilize the junta" and that they *in the government* were "the worst affected by the murders."

I almost laughed. But Maria just sighed and looked to the ground. She explained that anyone who tried earnestly to investigate the murder would be following in those women's footsteps. The women were found in the Archdiocese of San Vicente, where the violent paramilitary group ORDEN ran numerous death squads. Recent "land reform" in San Vicente had unsurprisingly benefitted only the already-wealthy right wing. ORDEN would do anything to maintain their possession of the land.

Tom and I were about to start our meeting with Roger and John then, so Maria excused herself. She was really something. Listening to her talk drove home the danger of the situation we were entering, a danger she faced every day.

I felt like I was in a house of mirrors, with no exit in sight.

22

The meeting with Roger Morris and John Boyer was productive. I filled the two religious leaders in our tentative plan to piggyback Kim's expected hanging to our refusal to load arms to El Salvador on December 22. This was met with no hesitation. Kim's situation was little known to the U.S. public, so a job action for that alone would lack the community support needed to last even a week. I then moved onto the more radical part of our plan.

"There's something else. If Kim is hanged, we and our friends will refuse to work ROK ships."

This provoked a much more fraught response.

"Steve, don't you think that's a little impractical?" John demurred, "I mean, a more far-reaching refusal will make it much harder to gain support."

"That's why we're not going to announce the boycott in our wire to Korea."

"Then what does it matter? If they don't know about the potential boycott, then it isn't a useful threat."

I explained our theory that the local Kim committee contained informers and spies from the Korean CIA. "If we organize a meeting with them and explain, we could count on the bigwigs of the ROK learning what we and our friends would do if they hanged Kim."

John and Roger took a moment to consider what I was saying. Their faces slowly curved into approving smiles.

"Play their own spies against them," John said. "I like it."

"But this plan would be likely to work only if a whole lot of agents began to report the threat," Roger chimed in. "We'd have to plant it in a lot of different places where we feel KCIA agents will be present."

We spent the rest of the hour brainstorming groups we knew in Melbourne, Auckland, New York and Washington who could help spread the rumor. By the end of the meeting, what had seemed like just a crazy notion of Tom's and mine had become a plan. A plan John called, with a laugh, our "Have you heard this?" campaign.

As I drove home, the long-anticipated rain of that day finally arrived. It was such a beautiful city at night, with the street lights and neon signs hazy in the rain. I picked up some takeout and headed home.

I had a mountain of calls to make and was trying to decide who to contact first when that decision was made for me by the ringing phone. It was Doug Martin, the clerk from Pier 50 who'd given me copies of the paperwork for the *Tropic Moon*. He was calling from the hospital, where they'd had to take his son.

"Jesus Doug, is everything okay?"

"Yeah, yeah, he should be alright. Just a flu. But listen, I'm calling you about something else."

Hearing someone call while their kid was in the hospital really drove home to me how tough this job can be, and how dedicated the men on the right side of the fight were.

"It's official. At two p.m. Friday-that's *tomorrow*, we'll be getting more aid for the *Moon*."

I knew to expect this, but it still wasn't easy to hear. I thanked Doug and told him to get back to his son.

Next, I was going to call my reporter friend Jim Birch. But as I reached for the phone, it rang, and lo and behold it was Jim! From there, things got even stranger. He had called to ask if he could line up a photographer, and maybe even a video crew, to prepare for the Friday remembrance at the Mission San Francisco de Asis.

"You can Jim, but there might be a big hitch." I explained to him all about the FUPS and the danger of violence involved, and we agreed to touch base tomorrow.

Finally, I was able to place a call, and I got through to my comrade-in-arms Frank Spaulding at Local 10. Frank filled me in on the Margarito and Gus meeting about the corrupt union local up the coast.

"Everything we got from Anthony Alvarez is right, but I've got an even clearer picture now, and it's worse than we thought. The boss of the crooks is a guy named Tony Trestelli. Trestelli has been blackmailing members of the union with family in the Philippines to voice their support for Reagan, Marcos, and the gang-friendly union heads. Their families back home are being threatened, used as leverage. It's heavy stuff, Steve. I told them we'd do whatever we could to assist them. Gus is going to speak at the big union convention in two weeks."

"Sounds good. Did you give them my apologies?"

"Sure did. And they said how sorry they were that you hadn't been able to join us."

Frank and I then filled each other in on all the other events of the day. The two of us were like partners, and liked to keep the other one abreast of every development.

We hung up, and I was finally able to eat my takeout, which by this time had gone cold. I poured a vodka on the rocks and turned on the news. The whole show, all they talked about was a couple of fires at big hotels in Las Vegas and New York. There wasn't so much as a mention of the women in El Salvador. That really got my blood boiling. I decided to turn in for the night. As I lay in bed, my thoughts became increasingly concerned. If even four religious women getting murdered in El Salvador wasn't enough to make the news, how could we? Getting decent press was going to prove extremely difficult, no matter what support we had for our refusal.

23

Friday, December 5, 1980

As the alarm sounded, my dream vanished without a trace, and thoughts of the day to come rushed in. A day of work and worry and fog. For a moment I just lay there, listening to the patter of rain, considering the chaos I'd soon be facing.

After a quick breakfast and a cup of joe I was on the road. I drove to the corner of Taylor and Beach to pick up a *Chron*, where I found the headline the TV news had neglected to report:

"SALVADORANS KILL 4 U.S. MISSIONARIES."

I garnered a few new details from what Tom had told me. The missionaries had been shot in the back of the head with a large-caliber pistol. Execution-style.

"This time they won't get away with it," Robert White, the U.S. Ambassador to El Salvador, said when he spoke of the deaths.

I folded the paper and made my way into the union hiring hall, jumping over the numerous puddles between me and the building. It was 6 a.m. I made sure to be in early today so I could finish all my chores uninterrupted by dispatch time. It was Friday, which meant payday, which meant a flood of guys coming to me because they'd got shorted on their checks.

I started with a quick call to my union president. Paul told me he'd heard that the Reaganites were internally blaming the women for their own deaths. "Outside agitators," they called them. Typical.

Paul went on to say that, with the *Star* due in tomorrow, he should meet with Tom Augustine today. I agreed and said I'd get on the line to Tom by eight and set something up.

I checked my mail, did some tasks and checked in with Dolores about the local's weekly bulletin, and come six-thirty, the floodgates opened.

"Steve, I got shorted *again!*"

"Steve, these jerk-offs left me almost a whole day short."

"They thought I wouldn't notice five bucks."

"A *dollar*, Steve! A single lousy dollar for *two hours* driving lifts. And that should be at a skill rate, mind you."

I often wondered whether or not the shorting was deliberate. Not necessarily to hurt the guys (though it did that). Just to tie up the union with foolish nonsense. It could take me an hour or more to get back the shorted payment for a guy, even if it was as little as a buck or two. And by seven-thirty, six dockers had already reported being shorted. And that was the same as every payday. The bosses always insisted it was a mistake, but could they really make *so* many mistakes without it being on purpose?

Knowing Michael McSweeney would call soon to ask what I'd done about his beef, I wanted at least to give him the impression that I had actually done something. But every time I tried to open his paperwork, even more people were in my office talking about shorts. After handling a few of the reports, Dolores buzzed me and said McSweeney was on the line. Because I hadn't gotten to his stuff yet, I thought I would just let him stew for a while.

I asked Dolores to tell him I'd gone to the hall, and she would ask me to call him when I returned. I also asked if she would mind digging through our bulletin and finding anything it had said about El Salvador. As usual, she and Shirley were ten steps ahead. She said they'd been filing pieces ever since the coup last October and she could have them on my desk by eight thirty. What troupers.

I called Al Richards, steward at Pier 15, to check in on the situation with the ear-splitting lifts and confirmed I'd be over at nine to check how testing was going. He sounded cheery as he filled me in:

"I got here at seven and learned that the two lab guys were here and at work by six. They really knew their stuff and were ready to test. The drivers seemed pretty pleased when I showed them what they'll be driving. All in all, my report is ten-four."

"Great to hear that, Al," I said. "I'll see you at nine and we can piss off Montieth again."

"Ha! Looking forward to it."

We both laughed, and I moved onto my other business. Frank had written in today's union bulletin that there'd be a gathering in the church to commemorate the killings of the women in El Salvador. Al Richards said he was real sorry he couldn't make it, but his wife was still sick. I told him I was sorry on both those counts.

Next, I was on the line to Doug Martin, the clerk at Pier 50. It wasn't news I was hoping to hear. He still had no idea what exactly the additional "safety and rescue gear" scheduled to be rebooked to the *Star* consisted of. I told him to keep his eyes sharp and get back to me soon as he had anything concrete.

Now I finally had some time to look over McSweeney's papers properly. By rights, his business was next. To keep the pressure on his side, I made sure to call him before he could call me back.

"Well, I promised I'd call by ten."

"But you don't know what's going on here, Morrow."

"Then why don't you explain it to me?"

"You won't get it unless you come down here yourself!"

"I'm doing the best I can, but at the earliest, I'll be there Monday morning." I added, "Look, Michael. I see where you're coming from. We've got to strengthen your hand somehow, right?"

That gave him pause.

"I… guess so?"

"So, to cover your ass, tell them you've already told me a dozen times they can't decide what to do until I come down. And tell them I said that if they don't decide soon, I might just cite them. What do you think OSHA might say when it sees your 'documentation'?"

"Woah, Morrow! There's no need to get OSHA involved in this." McSweeney knew that if OSHA got involved, they'd see that our safety code was less specific than theirs, and that could lead to hefty fines.

"Just tell them what I said."

"Ugh, fine. But did you take a look at my stuff?"

I assured him that I had, and told him which of the suggested repairs would be suitable.

"Right. The most expensive fix to install," McSweeney said. "Shocking."

"Well, you tell your side that if they don't do their job right, our next meeting will be on the picket line."

I pushed a button beside my phone that made a buzzing sound, not unlike an intercom. I'd had it installed for situations just like this.

"Hold it," I said to the empty space in my office. I told McSweeney I had another call I had to take and wished him luck.

As I chuckled to myself, Frank poked his head into my office. "What's cooking, soldier?" he said.

I told him I thought his bulletin was terrific. He told me to come in and have a coffee with him when I could, he had more news on Margarito and Gus. I told him I just had to call Tom Augustine and then I'd be right in.

When I reached Tom, I told him that Paul would be at our next meeting on the South Korean situation. "If it can be arranged," I went on, "he'd also like to talk with you before the gathering Maria's organizing."

"Of course," Tom said, "but why?"

"I've learned that it looks like they're speeding things up on the aid shipment by rebooking some stuff to the *Tropic Star*, a sister ship of the *Moon*, which starts loading at eight tomorrow morning."

I thought that would give Tom some pause. And it did.

"With all the talk of suspending aid, they're trying to get it all out as quick as possible. Which means we may have to go the more drastic route. A wildcat strike. Paul just wants to make sure you and your associates know in advance what might happen."

Tom took a moment to gather his thoughts, then responded: "Okay. How about we talk about the Kim situation until six, and then Paul can have the floor for the rest of the meeting?"

"Terrific," I said. Tom told me that preparations were going well for the gathering tonight at the Mission San Francisco de Asis. I said I was glad, that it was sure to be a dramatic and moving affair.

Tom's intercom buzzed and he said he had to run. I joked to myself that maybe he had a secret button by his desk as well.

24

As I walked into the office of our newsletter editor Frank Spaulding, I wished I'd read more on Marcos and the Philippines, a political climate about which I knew very little. Right now El Salvador was our most pressing concern, but it felt good knowing I belonged to a union that stood up to injustice everywhere. Besides, Margarito and Gus were our brothers. Their struggle was our struggle.

Frank said the focus on their meeting had been security. For the past year or longer, pro-Marcos agents had been infiltrating their anti-corruption, anti-Marcos group in one of our West Coast Locals. As a result, the fascist sympathizers often knew what the group had planned, and their meetings and rallies were regularly disrupted. Sometimes these conflicts even got physical. What's more, files, records, and mailing lists, as well as supplies, equipment, and cash, had all gone "missing" from the local's offices. Folks were followed, phoned at night, harassed. Sometimes even children had been threatened at school.

"Christ." I shook my head.

"I know. Can you believe it?"

Frank asked me for an update. I told him it was looking more and more likely that the first shipment would start loading tomorrow. Saturday. A fog of uncertainty hung over both our heads as I left the room, unable to predict what even the next 24 hours might hold.

"Roll with the punches, ay pal?" Frank reassured me as I walked out the door.

That fog followed me all the way to Pier 15, hanging over my head in the gray city skies. But once I saw Al Richard's waving hand, my mind cleared. I had a job to do.

Al introduced me to the lab guys who were testing the lifts. They tried to tell me that they'd fitted the lifts with a decibel meter to see how noisy they were. But you hardly needed a decibel meter, the lifts were so loud I couldn't hear a word the guys were saying!

I went inside to find Montieth in his regular perch, his big feet up on his big desk. He raised his ham-hock hand almost as if to shoo me away. I decided to lift the mood a little: "Everything looks good to me! When do you think you'll get the results?"

His shaggy brows sunk into a deeper frown. "It's costing real dough. And it's a weekend lab that'll run into Sunday night," he grumbled, his voice like the rasping of rocks on a metal shovel.

"But think of all the dough you're going to make! Well, assuming it all works out."

"And if not?"

"Well then I *know* your top priority will be to ensure the safety of your workers and reduce the noise level as per OSHA standards."

That really stuck in his craw.

"Let's just see what the lab says," I told him.

Having shown face and said I'd be back Monday to hear the results, I next bolted over to Pier 32. John Tilby told me that to his surprise, the bosses were actually doing the right thing. The lifts they stopped were hauled to the shop for repair and, just in case they encounter more problems, they were draying some more lifts over from 27.

"And here I've been expecting them to fool around!" I said. "I think soon it'll be time to make the same push to reduce noise on the tractors and jitneys. The bosses are on the run, so why not move to rattle their cage right now?"

"I like the sound of that!"

I stuck my head into Webster's office to congratulate him on a job well done, but he seemed pretty sore about the whole thing.

Next was the check-in I was most nervous about: Doug Martin and the shipment of arms. Doug greeted me with an excited grin and told me he had good news–the additional "safety and rescue equipment" bound for El Salvador wouldn't arrive until next week! I said that was terrific and he showed me his paperwork on the case. It was darned good work.

I used Doug's phone to call my answering service. Tom had phoned to say his contact in DC, Father Berger, was reporting a growing buzz about a suspension of aid. As it turned out, this was an understatement. I got a beep from Paul, and when I picked it up, he told me the State Department had announced a suspension of aid!

"They said there is 'some evidence' that a junta force may have been involved in killing those women. All aid has been halted, cut or suspended. Economic aid will be limited to twenty million dollars and nonlethal military aid at another five."

"What does that mean for us?"

"It's unclear. There's been no talk about shipments already in the pipeline."

In just the past hour, it felt like things were really swinging our way. But I reminded myself that last time, when they suspended aid to Chile, they still tried to force us to load the existing aid. I didn't see why this time would be any different.

Just when I thought the good news couldn't keep coming, Al phoned me up from Pier 15. He said the lab guys' tests reported the noise of each lift as exceeding ninety-two decibels. Which meant the drivers' exposure could not exceed six hours.

"That's great!" I cheered. "That proves what we already knew."

"But that's not all. Montieth freaked out. He said the tests are no good without explaining why. He said the guys from the hall 'got the testing machines all fucked up on purpose.' He fired them, Steve! And now he's threatening to fire us if we make a fuss."

And there it was. The other shoe had dropped.

25

Montieth's childish stunt was likely to tie me up until the gathering this evening. When a firing occurs over a safety dispute, it was my job to establish all the facts and arbitrate. Anxiety washed over me. The day was getting out of hand and I still had a million things to do. I told Al I'd be down as soon as possible and hung up.

I called Frank and asked him to handle some things I was hoping to deal with. I was supposed to talk to the stewards. If any of them called, I asked Frank to tell them they could reach me at Pier 15.

"Will do, buddy."

I raced back up the waterfront and got to Pier 15 just after 1:10. Montieth was standing there with something I'd never seen on him before–could it be?–a smile. I tried to suppress my anger so he wouldn't see me as being on the back foot, saying, "I hear you've done a really dumb thing."

"I couldn't wait in your little line no more, Morrow. So I had to do something to get you here right away."

"Wait a second." I tried to fight the rage bubbling up in me. "Are you telling me you *aren't* firing anyone?"

"Nope. A little joke, I guess."

"If that's your idea of a joke, I think I'll stick to the funny pages."

"Well you're here, aren't you?" His smug grin curled up further. He looked better frowning.

"Let me tell you something about your little joke. I was supposed to meet with the stewards this afternoon. Now I've told them I'll be tied up here, so they've got to come all the way down. Let's see if they think your joke's funny. Or call McSweeney, who's been trying to get a hold of me the guts of two days. See if he laughs. Who knows? Pretty soon you might just get a reputation for yourself as a comedian."

That wiped the smirk right off his face.

I went to check in on Al, who apologized profusely.

"Once Montieth heard you were coming back, he changed his mind! But I thought if I called you again to tell you to forget it, he might just go through with the firings anyhow."

"You did the right thing, Al. Don't sweat it."

I told him the stewards would be coming by and he showed me to a desk I could use. My first call there was from the traveling steward, Harvey Garrison. Harv had always been active in the union. He arrived on the waterfront in 1959 and was elected to our Executive Board in 1964, when he was first eligible to run. Every year after that he had been reelected, and he was still serving. In 1968 he was elected to our Board of Trustees and as a convention delegate. He had set an example in every way and was a crackerjack.

"Steve Morrow! It's been too long, old friend."

He told me Frank had filled him in on the entire situation and he was ready for action. I said that was great to hear, then told him about Montieth holding me up here and said I'd be in touch with him as soon as possible.

"Well, I'm just in Carlo's, I can get down there whenever you want me." Carlo's on Green Street was a favorite longshore haunt of Harv's.

"Thanks, Harv. I've reached out to Howie Rutherford, Hank Lorenz and Axel Peck. Let's see if we can't get all of us in a room together to talk this thing out."

Right at that moment, my beeper sounded.

"That's Howie now," I told Harv. "I'll let you know what he says."

"You know where to find me."

Howie told me he read in the morning *Chron* about the four women, and that it was terrible.

"Right. But partly because of all that, I've got to see you and the other stewards for the *Star*. There's no easy way to say this, but it looks like arms for the junta might be shipped on her."

Howie wasted no time. "Frank tells me you're cleaning up some mess on Pier Fifteen. Is that right?"

"Yeah."

"I can be there in ten."

"Don't kill yourself! Make it fifteen."

I called Harv to let him know Howie was coming down. Both of them were with me within fifteen minutes. I still hadn't heard back from Hank and Axel, but I figured this couldn't wait any longer.

"Thank you both for coming down so fast," I said. "I know this isn't the best of circumstances, but it's good to see you."

"Any time, Steve," Harv replied.

"Yeah, and this is of huge importance," Howie added. "If they're planning on shipping aid from our coast, that's something we've gotta act on immediately."

I had built up a whole spiel in my head to try get the stewards on board with a wildcat. Information about the living situation in El Salvador: 40% unemployment, 16% employment year-round, an average daily wage of $1.50, one in four children dying before age five, average life span of forty-six years, and 80% of the population without electricity, water, and sanitation. An appeal to our ethical responsibility to offer support, and a detailed account of the potential impact our refusal could have on American aid shipments to fascist regimes in general.

But as I started on it, I could see my spiel was unnecessary. Howie and Harv were already well versed on Salvadoran politics and in full support of whatever action we deemed necessary. I knew I had Frank's bulletin to thank.

At that point Hank called to say he was completely tied up and wouldn't be able to get down until this evening. Damn. That was no good for me.

As he often does, Harvey came through in a pinch. He said that Hank–and Axel, if he reached out–could come by his place for a meeting at 6:30, where he'd catch them both up to speed. Their enthusiasm to take action reassured me that with such good men, if anyone could actually win this fight, it would be us.

I checked my watch and figured I should check in on the lifts situation. I suggested that while I was gone, Harvey and Howie might study the booking paperwork and a pack of snaps, which I gave them.

There wasn't much left to say to Harv and Howie. I told them I'd know when to move because I'd get a tip on the shipment from Doug Martin, a clerk at Pier 50. We agreed all of us should meet with Doug later in the day for coffee to fine-tune our plans. I also said Jim Birch from the *Chronicle* would probably want to speak with them both once things kicked off. They said that was just fine and we gave our usual sign-off:

"Keep the faith."

"And watch the game, brother."

As I walked towards Montieth's office, Al came up to me and said the boss had relented. The guys would finish work at 2:30 today and they'd rent some lifts until these ones were up to standard. Al said he knew I was due over on Pier 32, so there was no need for me to see Montieth again. But I couldn't help myself.

"Hey Joe. You made a good call there."

But Montieth just grumbled and tapped away at his ancient adding machine, I assume adding up all the money he was spending.

26

As I left Al Richards at Pier 15, I realized the day had really gotten away from me. It was after four already and I hadn't eaten. I quickly stopped off at Red's takeout on the way to Tom Augustine's office at the Archdiocese and munched on a sandwich in the car.

Paul, Reverend Roger Morris & Minister John Boyer were already seated in a semi-circle of easy chairs when I arrived. Tom greeted me from his desk. They were talking about the Washington response to the Maryknoll murders, and asked me for any updates. I remained standing as I spoke.

"President Carter claims he is sending a group to El Salvador to investigate. But I'm skeptical. The head of the investigation will be William D. Rogers, a Reagan man. And get this–he'll be reporting to both Carter *and* Reagan. How's that for impartial?"

The guys shook their heads.

"Ambassador White talks a big talk, but when he met with the junta he fell back on the old formula, expressing our 'shock and outrage.' That sentiment has been repeated so often it seems meaningless. He got another classic formula back, offering 'profound regrets.' In short, the traditional channels are going nowhere, and our direct action is looking as necessary as ever."

When I finished, Tom asked me to talk for a while about the Kim situation and our plans. I told them our idea to leak our threat to stop shipping to ROK and asked Roger and John for their assistance. In addition to being members of Tom's church group, they both served as consultants to a group called the Academic Sector of the San Francisco Regional Branch of the U.S. Committee for Kim. Which, unfortunately, was permeated with KCIA operatives. They could get friends to call the local Kim branch to ask if folks there had heard the whispers of a boycott of Korean goods. The timing and the callers could be changed and shuffled to obscure the identity of individuals and groups making the calls, sowing rumors at lots of events and places where agents of the ROK would surely hear them.

John said that at nine the next morning, a small but important group of religious people, who could sow the rumors as I had suggested, would be meeting with Kim supporters in New York. In the next week similar meetings would take place in Boston, Chicago, Philadelphia, Seattle, and L.A. In each city, he could call a friend or two to say we had just heard that if Kim is hanged, the foreign outlets for ROK trade are going to be disrupted, and ask them to check out that rumor. If the union wanted, he and Roger could start spreading the word as soon as five o'clock today.

When John paused, Paul looked around the room for comments. Once we all waved him off, he said: "Well men. Let's get to it."

At that moment, however, my beeper went off. I stood, saying it could be something important. But it turned out to be just one of the guys who had been shorted calling to thank me for helping him out. I quickly went back to the meeting to find Tom finishing up a phone conversation.

"I'll be sure to report this at the gathering this evening at the Mission. Let's stay in touch. Thanks from everyone here."

Tom put down the phone and grimaced.

"That was a contact of mine in the budget department. I got in touch with him when I first heard of the aid shipment to ask about that bogus 'Safety and Rescue' classification. He just confirmed that the stuff is in fact *entirely* weapons related. What are called 'public safety implements' are actually lethal weapons, including the M-1 rifle and M-2 carbine; the .45 twelve-gauge pump-action shotgun; the M-14, M-15, and M-60 light machine gun. All of these are technically classed as 'non-lethal'."

We were all enraged, but glad we finally knew what we were dealing with. The Department of Defense might have tried to pull the wool over our eyes with that S&R deception. But now if they tried it, we'd nail them.

With that we broke the meeting so John and Roger could get to work planting seeds.

27

Paul and I stuck around for Tom's meeting of the Social Justice Commission, which was a lot bigger than usual. Almost all the members of his regular monthly meeting were there, and most of them had brought a friend or two, many of whom were clergy. *Word must be getting around,* I thought.

After some brief opening statements, Tom invited Paul to speak to the group. Paul stood up, looked around the room, and cleared his throat.

"First of all, on behalf of the union, I'd like to express my condolences about the tragic murder of those four nuns. The union is honored, and I am personally honored, to be working alongside the clergy for justice and peace in El Salvador.

"Many of you have probably heard talk of a suspension of aid. We at the union would like to have our say to you before any official announcement is made. It now appears likely that some of the equipment in the shipment has been rebooked to an earlier ship. Washington announced today that *they* would be suspending aid to El Salvador. Unfortunately for us, however, that announcement does not affect cargo already in the pipeline.

"We have two friends working together in DC: Tom's budget pal, Father Anthony Berger, and our union's rep in Washington, Mike Garvey. We think this so-called suspension is just a public relations move. When first spoken of, it was to last only until the junta proved it wasn't involved in the killing of the nuns. But we just found out that the 'investigation' into these killings is being carried out by a staunch Reagan ally. We would be shocked if they came back confirming the junta's involvement. The only option we are left with is to outright refuse to ship arms."

At that moment May Burnet, the switchboard worker, said that Father Berger and Mike Garvey were on the phone and needed to speak with Paul and Tom. He excused himself, gestured to me and said: "As for the details of the wildcat, I leave you in good hands."

While he was gone I distributed Frank's bulletin and talked about the need for public support in order for this wildcat to have a hope. We agreed that if a wildcat went ahead this Saturday, we'd meet again then to further discuss strategy.

Paul came back in the room. He said that Tom was still on the phone, but he had more news from Garvey.

"It's exactly what we thought. There's a struggle going on between the Carter camp and the Reagan camp, and the Carter folks are losing. In spite of the suspension, any aid in the pipeline is set to continue. And the Rogers investigation is going to last a measly two days!"

This provoked mutters of indignation from the room.

"Apparently as a compromise," Paul continued, "the junta is going to undergo some minor cosmetic changes, a PR shift to centrism. But Duarte will stay on as leader and will soon be installed as president. Meanwhile, another member of the junta, a deeply conservative hawk named Colonel Jaime Gutierrez, will be installed as vice president and commander-in-chief. Ostensibly in this new arrangement Duarte will have no power over the military, but the whole thing is baloney."

"When will all this happen?" a concerned voice in the room asked.

"Next Friday. When the report comes in. Which is also when the suspension of aid will end. And there's more. Father Berger has confirmed that the junta needs the radio equipment in this very shipment to be able to launch its new offensive. That's why they're pushing so hard not to suspend it."

Paul had to make some calls about these new developments, so I closed with a few statements about our 'Safety and Rescue Equipment' discovery and told everyone I'd see them at the Mission to remember the slain Maryknoller nuns and others killed by the death squads.

28

Despite being born and raised in Frisco, I had never been inside Mission San Francisco de Asis, more commonly known as the Mission Dolores. I often drove past it, but now walking inside, I could see that the interior was alive with color, far more color than any church I had ever been in. The lighting was indirect and softly muted, delicately hitting off the elaborate murals. This was the perfect place to hold the gathering for the nuns.

The chapel was crowded, and when I walked through that throng of people, I came upon a basilica twice the size of the chapel that was even more crowded. Standing in the line, I soon saw our own Dolores and Frank. They told me Paul was holding a seat for me. I spotted many folks I know as I walked over to my seat. It filled me with a sense of reassurance and belonging.

Paul informed me as I sat that our folks had volunteered to sit in the chapel because it was feared that with all the support, there wouldn't be enough room for refugees in the basilica. I looked around again at all the familiar faces, proud.

As the lights dimmed, the church became a jumbled, swirling scene. An altar boy came from each side of the altar to light the candelabra flanking it. With that, and a choir singing a lilting song, the buzz and stir were dampened, the lights dimmed further, and the singing ended. Father McGinnis walked slowly to the altar rail, where he knelt and crossed himself. Following him was Sister Catherine Anne, who had just returned from El Salvador.

Father McGinnis began by reading a note from the Archbishop for San Francisco, who had been called to Washington for a similar memorial mass.

"Since the Archbishop of El Salvador, Oscar A. Romero, was shot and killed by a death squad, over eight thousand more people have been slain. So now, as the Salvadorans have done so often before, we have gathered to honor a few recent martyrs for freedom and human rights. While I am very sorry not to be there with you, I would like Father McGinnis to start—as is the practice among Salvadorans—by reciting the archbishop's name. All of you who are here will respond with a firm and joyous, 'Presente'."

After a solemn pause, the Father began:

"Oscar A. Romero."

"Presente!" The ringing unison sounded to me both joyous and anguished, in equal measures. Father McGinnis continued with a long list of other martyrs recently lost to the violence. After each one, the crowd sounded off with another strident "Presente!" The pain never left their voices, but as the chorus went on it grew increasingly defiant and united, until it sounded like one booming voice resonating throughout the Mission halls.

"PRESENTE!"

When the cries finished, you could hear people beginning to stir. Some of them coughing, some clearing their throats, some wiping their eyes, and many quietly weeping. After such a loud eruption, it was deeply affecting to hear so many individual emotional responses in such an intimate quiet.

Next, Sister Catherine took to the pulpit. She was keeping it together, but you could see a well of pain beneath her eyes.

"I just returned from the Libertad Mission in El Salvador and must call to the four dear sisters." Again, their names were spoken one after the other.

"Maura Clarke."

"Presente!"

"Ita Ford."

"Presente!"

"Dorothy Kazel."

"Presente!"

"Jean Donovan."

"Presente!"

These cries were far more fragmented, as some people began to break down into outright sobs. Next, Father McGinnis invited anyone in the crowd to add a name to the call. With so many people directly affected by the violence in El Salvador, there were many names called out from the congregation. As they did so, we all regathered our strength and joined together in an ever-more-insistent "Presente!"

After the last name was called, another haunting silence hung in the air. Father McGinnis slowly nodded.

"So shall it be for now."

Father McGinnis then invited us to close the vigil by singing "We Shall Overcome." With the words "May God be with you" he led us in the somber, hopeful song.

As we sang, he and Sister Catherine made their way through the aisles. I had tried my best to keep it together throughout the ceremony, but as Sister Catherine passed my row, I didn't try to hide the tears rolling down my face.

29

Outside the chapel, I locked eyes with Frank, our newsletter editor. The two of us nodded in silent agreement that the event had really been something. Something perversely nice about an event like this is that it brings so many people you know together, and I found myself speaking to numerous old buddies from the union. About the event, and the situation, but also about fishing and old dockers stories.

One special thing happened as I was talking to Doug Martin, who was there with his wife. Paul Murphy, who was twenty feet away, overheard me say Doug's name. He ended his conversation, came over and greeted Doug like a close, long-lost pal. He beamed, shook Doug's hand, and patted his arm before turning to Doug's wife and bowing. He said that her husband was doing a hell of a fine job, then told Doug to keep up the good work. Coming from our union president, I knew it meant a lot to Doug. And his wife.

I tried to find Jim Birch from the *Chronicle*, but I couldn't spot him in such a large crowd. But a large group was forming around Paul and Doug, and it was good to hear what all the union guys thought of the gathering.

"The politics of it are darned good," Joe Margolis said. Being as staunch an atheist as he was, I was glad it had still moved him. He made a point I had never heard of.

"Leaving religion aside, politically speaking this gathering is a lot better than what's coming from the so-called House of Labor." Joe meant the AFL-CIO, which usually either sat on its hands or actively supported the reactionary foreign policy of the US government.

After a fun but all-too-brief catch up, I said I'd have to go home if I wanted to be in fighting trim for tomorrow, then went to pay my respects to Father McGinnis, Sister Catherine and Tom. They were surrounded by people, so I made it quick and then headed off.

I got home at 9:30 and checked my messages. There was one from Hank, so I checked in to see how the meeting with the stewards had gone. Everyone was still there when I called, including Axel, so I knew they had been productive. I got them up on the developments since we had last spoken and we agreed to see each other in the morning. I left a message on Paul's machine to let him know the stewards from the *Star* were all set if we had to ask them to walk off the job rather than load the weapons.

Next Jim Birch called me. He said he'd been looking for me at the vigil, too. He said he'd been moved by the "historic crowd of union and religious folk, and the numerous cultures and ages represented at the service. As tragic as the event was, it's going to be great for the piece I'm working on."

I told him I was happy to hear that and went through the list I'd made of relevant developments for him, especially Tom's memo on the Safety and Rescue equipment. By the time we finished talking it was 11:00pm.

I turned on the Channel 4 news, which opened with the suspension of what was still being called "the junta aid." They spent a large portion of the segment talking about William Rogers' "truth-seeking mission" and "search for answers." Then there was a brief account of the lives of the four women.

Well it's about time, I thought, switching the TV off and falling in to bed.

I was asleep before the ship's bell sounded midnight.

30

Saturday, December 6

The Tick Tock Cafe was unusually quiet for a Saturday morning, the parking lot empty of the long-haul rigs and delivery trucks that make up its usual clientele. I sat at their trademark horseshoe-shaped counter, nursing a cup of joe with a picked-at bear claw on a plate next to me, feeling groggy as all hell. My alarm had been set for 5:15, but I woke with a start to find it was only 4:15. My head was racing and getting back to sleep seemed unlikely, so I did some paperwork and came down here early.

I leafed through the morning's *Chronicle*. A lot about the government stalling aid, mostly what I already knew. The junta's deception had only deepened, and they were now categorically claiming that they had nothing to do with the nuns' murders.

The piece went on to report that the junta, at U.S. Ambassador White's insistence, would seek a "decisive showdown" with "the rightist military" and that five million dollars of what was said to be "non-lethal military aid" was being withheld until the junta could prove that its forces were not involved in killing the women. I was glad the story was getting press, but I didn't like the conservative, overly trusting tone. A lot of people reading this would believe that the investigation was being handled in good faith.

Soon I was joined by the four stewards and Doug Martin, as planned. Doug introduced himself to everyone and we chose a window booth as our battle station for the morning.

"Have you seen this?" Harvey said, holding up today's *Chron,*

"With press like this, today ought to be a cakewalk."

We smiled wryly at this remark. Once everyone had ordered and settled in, we got down to business. First, I reminded the stewards that we were to keep mum about the aid until there was a rebooking.

"Remember, the plan is still to announce refusal on the twenty-second of December. Everything today is just in case they try to sneak by us and try to load the gear on the *Star* or the *Wind*."

Then I filled them in on the mislabeled "safety and rescue" equipment.

"Once we announce the refusal, the government might come out with this lie about the cargo. But they don't know we know what's really inside. So if they try to pull something, we'll hammer them."

After that necessary prelude, we got into the mechanics of the plan.

"As the clerk at Pier 50, Doug will be the first to know if there's an order to load. If there is, he'll give me a beep first, then let each of you know. Then it's go time. If by noon they don't order us to load the arms, you should call me—but not too many of you. One or two at most. We want to keep this quiet."

"Yeah, people could get suspicious, the six of us all calling on a Saturday like this," Howie Rutherford said.

"If anyone asks, tell them I had a beef with McSweeney about a faulty crapper during the week," I replied. "Say I asked you guys to keep an eye on things."

"Ha, I like the sound of that."

It was now 7:10 in the morning.

"Is there anything else to discuss?" I asked. Everyone shook their head in the negative.

"Good luck, guys. Today could be the day. And there's no one I'd rather be in this thing with."

"Thanks, Steve."

We all sat there in silence for a moment, some of us glancing at our papers. Eventually Harvey raised his head: "So, what now?"

"Now, we wait."

After that, everybody seemed to loosen up, and the conversation started to flow. More dockers started to flood in as we ate, and pretty much everyone who came in knew at least one man sitting at my table. The Tick Tock was a sea of smiles and shaking hands as people caught up and shot the breeze.

As I looked on and admired the fellowship, I was struck with a flash of how this same scene had repeated over the years. I'd been coming to the Tick Tock since I was a fresh-faced kid. Back then, nothing used to give me more joy than a laugh and a drink with a buddy from the dock. So many folks, back then and right here, had fashioned good lives for themselves. From their work, their companionship, their union bond. It brought a faint nostalgic smile to my face. But at the same time, it struck me that I didn't really feel like a part of this crowd anymore. More of an observer. I could clearly see my face laughing along with these men, but that face seemed like a ghost to me.

I decided to dip out and head to the office. I said goodbye to my breakfast companions and wished them the best of luck in today's fight, then got into my car and pulled away.

31

There was a message from Tom waiting for me at the office. I called him up.

"Paul asked me to call you with the latest news from Father Berger and Mike Garvey," he said. "Could you take some notes?"

"The pen's already in my hand, pal."

He began by reading me the information from a document prepared by the Institute for Policy Studies titled "Background Information on El Salvador and U.S. Military Assistance to Central America." It listed military aid already sent to El Salvador. Under "Safety and Rescue Equipment" was listed: items for riot control (tear gas, helmets, and flak jackets); weapons parts; weapons spares, components, and accessories.

"This is perfect. Now we have actual documented proof of what they claim is 'safety equipment'. How did we get this?"

"Father Berger has some... connections. But listen Steve, that makes it all the more important that we don't use this information without a union discussion."

"You got it."

Tom said he had to go and we hung up. I worked for a couple of hours on getting my notes and files of these developments all up to date– for now at least. Things were moving so fast that generally, by the time I'd written something down thirty more things had happened.

As I finished up I got a beep from Doug Martin at Pier 50. I picked up the phone and dialed.

"Well, what's the word?"

"I've been 'elected' to be the one to tell you. There hasn't been even a hint of rebooking. It's not happening today."

Relief coursed through my body. I thanked Doug and told him to have a great day, then hung up.

In quick succession I called Paul, Frank, Tom and all of the stewards with the good news: no confrontation today. No wildcat. They all said they were feeling good and ready for more. I mean, we all knew the *Wind* was due to be worked on Friday the 19th, just 13 days away. I was blown away by their willingness to stay the course and take on the PCMA and the government and thanked them for their commitment to the cause.

Hanging up the phone, I took a look around my empty office. For the first time since this whole business kicked off, I had nothing I needed to do right away. It was Saturday, I was "off duty." I stood up, grabbed my Filson, and went home.

***

I awoke to the sound of a ringing phone. It was 4:50 in the afternoon. I must've passed out as soon as I'd gotten back, because I was still in my jacket. It was Doug on the phone, calling me to say that the *Star* had just left the dock, *without* the aid.

"Now ain't that some news?" We both laughed.

As I talked on the phone, I looked out my window onto the San Francisco horizon and saw the *Tropic Star* steaming out to sea. I grabbed a pair of binoculars and gazed at the *Star*'s hazy afterdeck lights as she slowly disappeared into the mist beyond the Golden Gate bridge. Happy to see her go, but anxious because I knew the *Wind* was out plowing the Pacific on its way to Pier 50, San Franciso.

The fight was far from over.

32

Monday, December 8

With the *Star* having shipped off and Roger Morris and John Boyer sowing rumors about the Korea boycott, Sunday had been the closest I'd come to a day off in a long while. I actually woke up excited to do my house chores– something I never thought I'd hear myself say! It was a much needed rest. Come Monday morning I felt like I was ready for Round Two.

As Paul had predicted, the junta's most liberal member, Col. Adolfo Majano, had been ousted by the military and replaced by a Col. Jaime Gutierrez, said to be a fellow conservative. The *Washington Post* called it "another victory for the right."

As I suspected, McSweeney called me up almost as soon as I got into the office. He said he and his team had worked nearly to midnight and started again at six this morning making modifications to the *Pacific Thunder*.

"If we can tie things up by seven, the dockers should be able to start working at eight and finish loading by four." He sounded like he was reading from notes, his voice monotone with none of his usual hogwash. I decided to play innocent to get a better read on him.

"That sounds okay, but when do you figure I should show?"

His tone flipped.

"Well quite frankly, with all the work we're doing no one gives a goddamn no more."

I knew then they had decided to go with the shipwide-frame

I had recommended. Otherwise, a remark like that could be really bad for him.

"I'll be a son of a bitch. And after I put in all that effort to be able to see you today! What a shame." I could practically hear him seething. "Well, I'd better not get another call about a safety grievance."

"Don't worry, you won't."

Next, I got a call from over at Pier 32 confirming that the tractors and jitneys were getting repaired over there too and would be back on the dock by Thursday. Everything seemed to be going so smoothly. I should've been delighted. But a pit was growing in my stomach. Whenever things were going too well I got a bad feeling like that, as though something terrible was just waiting around the corner.

I checked in with Shirley and Paul. Everything seemed to be going smoothly over there. Then I put in a call to Roger and John. They'd spent Sunday calling contacts all over America, as well as even further afield. It was even better than I could've hoped. I called Doug Martin and Nick Rowan at Pier 50. The status was all quo. Still, that feeling in my stomach.

Finally, I decided to pay a visit to Frank, my brother-in-arms. I filled him in on all the calls I had made, the Labor Relations Committee paperwork I'd done between them, and some documents I'd written up on updating safety codes. As a joke I added:

"You know, one of these days we're going to have to have a talk about our division of labor here, Frank." He chuckled and said that it sounded like everything was in ship shape.

I hesitated, then decided to open up a little.

"That's just the problem, Frank. Everything's too quiet. It gives me this sense, that… that something's off."

The savvy editor took a moment to mull over what I had just

said. Then he told me something I chewed on for the rest of the day, and have continued to think about ever since. He told me about a young soldier during the Spanish Civil War who was anxious to go into battle. He was always asking his commander when they were going to get to fight. The commander, a seasoned veteran, said to the eager young man, "Those also serve who stand and wait." That young soldier was killed in battle a week later.

Frank didn't need to tell me the point of the story. I took out my folder on the junta aid situation, turned to a blank page and wrote a new heading: "Standing and Waiting."

So I stood and waited. I got a good night's sleep and awoke to a still waterfront. I fetched my daily *Chronicle*, and in there, things seemed to be quiet even in the El Salvador situation. Of course, I knew that wasn't the case. It was never quiet over there. There were just times we in the States chose not to listen.

My workday began with an enthusiastic call from the crew of the newly renovated *Thunder*. They said everything was top notch there and thanked me for my efforts. That left me feeling darned good.

There was a meeting of the Labor Relations Committee at ten (where the union and the bosses got to exchange "views"). I was reviewing my notes when Dolores came in with a mailer from Paul. It was the union's statement on the looming execution of Kim Dae-jung. And it was damn good. Powerful, full of pride, expressing exactly why it was essential that we show some solidarity. I thanked Dolores, grabbed my briefcase and headed out to a soggy morn.

The LRC meeting was at the Pacific Coast Marine Association building on Market Street. I showed up an hour early, partly to give me time for a final review of my files, and partly because the socializing before the meeting was a good time to sniff out some opportunities.

Sure enough, as I entered the reception lounge, I spotted a bird I'd been hoping to see: the company rep from "The Case of The Missing Meter Case." He was there to explain to his company why nearly a hundred longshoremen had called it a day at quarter to three under his supervision. Now, I knew he was going to try to pass the buck, so I decided to give him an opportunity not to do that.

I sidled up next to the guy and, in a hushed tone, said: "I have something you might want to look over if you want to keep your job."

He turned with a defensive frown, but agreed to go somewhere private. We went into a room across the hall, where I showed him my snaps.

"God damn," he sighed when he saw the case in the back seat. Right away he agreed to cop to it before the full meeting convened. He even thanked me for talking to him first.

Sure enough, when the meeting began the rep immediately agreed to pay our claim. The minutes read: "Investigation indicates that payment of this claim is in the company's interest." Well, that was a mild way of putting it.

The rest of the meeting was a mixed bag, winning some battles and losing some others. But I got a beep as we broke for the day from Al Richards, confirming that the new lifts on Pier 15 were passing the tests with flying colors. So overall I counted the day as a success.

That afternoon, I had to turn my attention back to Pier 50-B. But not for the junta arms shipments, for the crappers. I'd been using it as cover for my aid investigations for so long, I almost forgot it was a very real problem in and of itself. Still, it felt surreal handling business about toilets when I knew I was in such close proximity to a whole weapons arsenal.

Pulling up to the pier at 2:10, I spotted a sedan and a pick-up whose doors identified them as belonging to the Port of San Francisco. I took their presence as a good sign. And sure enough, as soon as I spotted McSweeney he introduced me to "three folks from the Port taking a look at them crappers." Their lead guy informed me that a crew had been at work replacing the toilets since seven this morning.

I asked McSweeney to show me around the facilities so I could put it in my record. It looked like good work, so I thanked the Port men, told the terminal boss I'd be back in a week to check in, and headed out. Well, at least we'd put out *one* fire in Pier 50-B.

After that, Frank and I met with our union's lawyers to discuss putting out the *other* fire. They explained to us some changes in the law that Reagan's people were working on to weaken OSHA protections for workers in lawsuits. They were very matter of fact about the whole thing. It felt like any other consultation over a worker dispute, even if it did spell out a lot of the legal troubles we were likely to face in the coming weeks.

Knowing that I'd face heavy traffic getting to the Bay bridge, I decided to head for home after stopping in Chinatown for takeout. Back home on the couch nursing a cold beer and some Mongolian beef, it occurred to me that I was getting back to the routine of my usual days. I mean, I took a lot of routine calls, did a lot of paperwork, but everything had been relatively easy to handle. It seemed, at least for now, I was settled quite nicely in my new role in what you might call "foreign policy affairs."

34

The news from El Salvador was in: José Napoléon Duarte Fuentes and Col. Jaime Abdul Gutiérez would form a new government by Monday, with Duarte president and Gutiérez the commander in chief. Col. Ramos, meanwhile, had been removed because he said on the radio that "military rightists" had infiltrated the government. As for the suspension of aid and the Rogers mission, Duarte said, "We reject any interference, wherever it comes from."

After reading the paper I took two calls, each of which brought good news. First, Tom Augustine told me word was getting around about our refusal to load; we were gaining a lot of support, especially after the gathering of remembrance Friday night. Then I heard from Roger and John, who said that ten of their friends–in Melbourne, Seoul, and Tokyo–had called to ask about a rumor they'd heard of a boycott of Korean ships. Everything was going according to plan.

Tom and Paul had organized an organizational meeting for today, and I entered the conference room feeling calm and collected. Walking in, I was met by a completely packed hall. Every chair, every couch in the vast space was occupied. There were even folding chairs taken out just for the occasion. I could see now that Tom was not exaggerating when he told me about the support we were getting.

Tom chaired the meeting, seated at the top of a T-shaped table in the center of the room, the International union officers to his right, the members of his Social Justice Commission to his left. He reported that, if there were no further surprises (I chimed in "no re-bookings"), we were tentatively scheduled to hold the blessing of the workers on Monday, December 22.

"Have those who were not here last week been sufficiently briefed?" Tom asked, kicking off the meeting. The crowd answered a resounding "yes."

The main outcome of the meeting, apart from really heartening everybody about the strength of our group, was that we decided to set up a group of subcommittees: a media committee, a blessing committee, a committee to build popular local support, a committee to gain support from the rest of the country, and finally, a committee to tie up any loose ends. I was in the loose ends committee.

Paul asked for volunteers and was met with a sea of hands. They divided the throng into the various committees. Agreeing to all check in the same time same place next week, all the committees went off to start to work. The operation was starting to feel like a well-oiled machine.

As there were no loose ends to tie up yet, I began to head out, when someone called over to me. Harold Painter, a friend of Tom's who was on the media committee, asked if he could have a word. I said sure and walked with him.

"I have a favor to ask, Steve," he began. "An exceptional sister from the AFL-CIO is doing a research project on struggles for social justice. You met her briefly at an event discussing Tara Hills. Susan Vogel."

Now, Tara Hills is a place where people burn crosses in the street every election season. A black brother in Local 10 had moved there recently with his wife and kids. Not only was a cross lit in front of their new dreamhouse–someone had even fired a shotgun round through their front door. Harold had introduced me to Ms.

Susan Vogel at a meeting of Tom's group to discuss what they could do.

Ms. Vogel was hired by the AFL-CIO to train people in public speaking and writing. Harold told me she was a staunch believer in the power of the written word to affect social change.

"She said she was interested in writing something about our struggle with the aid shipment," Harold said. "So, I ran it by Paul and Tom, and they gave it the okay."

"That's great."

"Well, I'm glad you think so. Because Paul suggested that you meet with her regularly to keep her up to date. We were also thinking maybe she could tag along with you sometimes with her camera. Follow your tenacious efforts for the stoppage."

"Whoa, whoa," I pulled back, reeling at the idea. But then I started to remember that Susan Vogel was a real knock-out. A beautiful face with thick sandy blonde hair. A dead ringer for Julie Christie in *Dr. Zhivago*.

"You know what Harry, I think that's a wonderful idea. Good for, um, the *cause*."

"Great! I'll tell her right away."

"Is she in town?"

"She's in the hall! Got into town last Tuesday, been staying with me and the wife. In fact, you should come to lunch with us."

Now, that was a lunch offer I couldn't refuse. We moseyed into the dining room together, and there, across the bustling room, peering down at a menu was the layered, luscious blonde bob of Ms. Susan Vogel.

She flashed her blue eyes across the room and gave me a bright smile, beckoning me over. She looked even prettier than I remembered. It took me a few minutes to recover from her attention, but once we got into the logistics of her stay, I managed to get a hold of myself.

"You can write for our union's monthly paper," I suggested, "or make reports and do camera work for our research department. If you want, I can take you up to Mission Rock Terminal where the aid is stored. That'd give you a real sense of the world of the dock."

To think, twenty minutes earlier I didn't even want the woman with me! Now I was bending over backwards to accommodate her every potential need.

"And, what should I wear?" she asked. I suggested a jumpsuit or tough pants, especially on the docks and ships. With boots and a cap.

"There's no need to spend big dough, but you might also want a raincoat."

She laughed and said: "To judge from what you're wearing, the strike uniform of 1934 is still favored, complete with West Coast Stetson."

I couldn't believe it. On my head was a white cotton cap with a visor we had called the 'West Coast Stetson' in honor of the longshore strike of '34. The fact that Vogel understood its significance to me and other longshoremen, and was even able to joke about it, amazed me.

"This cap," I chuckled, "is largely favored by those who are out of date, out of step and nearly out of gas."

Both Harold and Vogel laughed at that.

"Well, I have a rucksack with me complete with a jumpsuit, notebook, pens, camera, and film."

"I suppose you're ready to get to work, then."

I had to leave to handle some work on the Kim situation. As I started my goodbyes, Ms. Vogel asked when we might start. I said I didn't know but I'd give her a call real soon to let her know. I got out of my chair.

"Just one more thing, Steve," she said. I really had to go now, but her smile could've paralyzed me. "What do you figure the chances are of me getting back to my Chicago homestead in time for the Yuletide Season?"

"Well, if the cargo ends up on the *Wind*, we could win–or lose– by Christmas Day. But if the *Wind* just comes and goes, Washington won't change its mind between our refusal on the twenty-second and the day that old Santa shows up."

"Right now I have a red eye ticket for the twenty-third."

"I'd hold onto that, but maybe book another for Christmas Eve. Arbitration should take a break by then." With that, I said adios and got myself out of there.

It came as no surprise that as soon as I got rolling, my mind turned to Susan. As soon as I did, I swore to myself that I wouldn't even try. She was a serious sort. While she was in town, she needed to be able to do her work. Besides, I took her to be not a day over thirty, while I had just hit the big four-oh. I needed to remain principled and professional.

Now, this might already be obvious, but I was no Casanova. Truth is, I was focused on my work most of the time. Still, I had noticed that when ladies learned that I'd been widowed and had no kids, they had a tendency to get real friendly. I didn't think anything even close to that could come down with Susan, but as I drove through the overcast day, I found it awful hard to get her off my mind.

35

Friday, December 12

Another payday, another line of dockers outside my office reporting shorts. It was a regular day like any other, except it wasn't. Today was the day we learned the verdict of Kim's appeal. The date of his execution.

Thursday had tied me up all day with a dispute over at Local 10 about some winches, so I had a lot of work to catch up on today. But I was finding it hard to focus. The one saving grace with the Kim situation was that Roger and John's rumor campaign seemed to be working a charm. They told me they'd received thirty-one calls from six countries and nine major cities. Darned impressive stuff.

Even the El Salvador news was starting to get an eerie sense of normalcy. Everything was so messed up, but so consistent. It was starting to feel as regular as the lines of shorted workers every Friday. Twenty priests and nuns had begun a hunger strike. The appearance of only three members of the junta at a state function hinted at a purge. The US mission led by William D. Rogers had returned and found there was no "clear-cut" evidence linking the junta's security forces to the murder of the nuns. The mission findings recommended immediate resumption of aid "to help moderate forces gain the upper hand." Basically, it was a shit show.

About three hours into dealing with shortage complaints, the one thing that didn't seem to be getting shorter was the line outside my office. While talking to a guy who had been underpaid for the fifth week in a row, my phone rang. I looked at my clock. I knew what this was.

"Hello?"

It was Tom Augustine, saying Kim's execution was scheduled for Saturday, December 20th. 6 a.m. local time. In Frisco, that meant 1 p.m. on the 19th, a week from today. That's when they were going to kill him. I agreed to meet him at 12 pm at the Archdiocese and would ask my union president to join us.

***

I showed up at the Archdiocese ten minutes early, but still I found only one free easy chair left around Tom's desk. After somber nods and greetings, Tom asked for the latest on Kim. Everyone traded the run of the mill stories about the rumors spreading. But then Roger had the capper: he'd had an early morning call from a friend in Seoul who told him that a mole in the Korean CIA reported the agency had gone to "red alert" because of the union threats to refuse loading their ships!

Paul then read a draft of the telegram the union was preparing to send to Korean leader Chun Doo-hwan announcing our boycott threat. We agreed to leak the telegram next. Maybe we could really goose any spies into exposing themselves, which sure would be nice.

At 4 pm that afternoon, there was a summit at the International office to plan support for the arms refusal. I was going to give it a miss as I was confident I was up to date on all the latest information. But then it occurred to me that Ms. Vogel might be there. I told myself again that I wasn't going to try anything. Still, when I got in my car, I found myself driving up to the International.

My hopes were proven correct: Ms. Vogel was in attendance. But once again, Harold was with her. I just nodded and smiled. I was initially disappointed, but once I turned my attention to the meeting, I found that it was actually very interesting. There was a lot of talk on how to tally what could be fast-growing support.

Father McGinnis spoke on some of the logistics of the upcoming memorial service at the Mission for the victims of the death squads: the running order of the speakers, media invites, catering. All the unglamorous administration stuff that never gets talked about in the press but is essential to have down pat for any kind of collective action to run smoothly. This would be the public at large's first introduction to our cause. We knew it was essential to have every element of the event planned down to a tee.

It was a long and productive meeting, and I was glad I had come along. Afterwards, Paul asked if I wanted to grab dinner and catch up. He said he'd also invite Tom, Father McGinnis, Harold and Ms. Vogel. Well, now I was *real* glad I had come.

As Paul walked over to Tom, I turned and saw Ms. Vogel approaching me. She again flashed that smile that just seemed to melt everything around her.

"Things surely seem to be going well," she said.

"Ms. Vogel! Happy to see you here," I replied, trying to sound as casual as possible. Then she surprised me by saying:

"Please. Call me Sue, or Susan, and I'll call you Steve." She added that she wanted to hear all about my work on behalf of brother Kim. The perfect opportunity.

"Have you heard about Paul's dinner tonight? I'd be happy to give you some more details there."

"Oh. I..." She frowned and said that, as far as she knew, she, Harold and Tom were booked with Father McGinnis for an Archdiocesan dinner.

"You would be more than welcome to join us though, Steve."

Well, never have I been more annoyed to already have dinner plans. I gave her my apologies and said we should link up soon about her shadowing me.

After a pleasant but somewhat regretful bite with Paul and his crew at Tommy's Diner, I went home. I knew Frank had spent the day at a conference on the labor movement at Cal, the university in Berkeley, so I decided to call my old pal and check in on him. He said that he had really enjoyed talking with the student activists, that they were "darned good kids."

"Still Morrow, I gotta admit," he continued, "looking out there at their young faces, a part of me felt hopeless."

"Hopeless? About what?"

"The whole damn thing. Fighting the good fight. Sometimes it just feels like tilting at windmills."

"Well, you know what I'd say to that old friend."

"Oh yeah? What's that?"

"The same thing you say to me when I feel the same way: keep the faith."

There were two articles in the *Chron* about the junta: one from the AP and the other from the UPI. The first, at the top of page 26, said that in a reorganized junta of four, Duarte was president and Col. Gutierrez was vice president and "commander of the armed forces." The same article claimed that Duarte's appointments meant "a partial reduction of rightist influence in army leadership." It concluded that American economic aid would continue to be withheld, "pending significant restructuring of the government."

But what about the military aid! To me, the article was a load of horse crap, designed to muddy the account rather than clarify it, making Americans more confused about the situation and more likely to go along with whatever the powers that be decided to do.

The UPI article was a little better. It elucidated that Duarte had no control over the military; that the commander in chief was Gutierrez. Duarte's foes claimed he had "sold out to the army" because of his drive for power. They believe that with his move far to the right, he has become "a demagogue who thinks he is a demigod."

The article continued that he had recently blamed "a propaganda campaign by the communists, who control the world press," for the charges made against the military, insisting that the campaign was "a part of the conspiracy against Pinochet and Somoza, too." This, in my opinion, was a far more realistic character portrait of the leaders we were dealing with over there.

My work week started with a beep from Pier 35, our cruise ship pier. I called my pal Karl Scott over there, and the steward reported with a laugh that it was something pretty unusual. So I grabbed my Filson and headed over there.

Well I'll be damned if it wasn't one of the strangest disputes I'd ever had to settle. It all started when a big fruit shipment came in. The supervisors on 35 sent Karl over to see how many conveyor belts they'd need to unload it all. When he boarded and went to the locker where they'd be doing this work, he spotted a couple of boys–and I mean too young to shave–working the shipment.

Chuckling, he grabbed one of the glossy red Washington apples that always arrived with the Seattle fruit shipments. He took a bite of it and asked one of the kids, "So, how are folks in Norway?" Karl was proud to have identified the Norwegian flag on the ship, and he assumed these kids were enrolled in that nation's sea school.

The boy shrugged his shoulders and said, "Gee, I live in Oakland so I wouldn't know."

It turned out that the crew of about a dozen children belonged to the boys' club at a local church middle school! They'd been invited aboard the ship to have breakfast and gain some "work experience." Even worse, the boy Karl had been talking to was their supervisor!

The dockers were all pretty steamed. I really lit into the terminal boss, the stevedore rep, and two clowns from the PCMA. I mean, foreign crews were one thing, but this ship was literally using child labor! The unwarranted reassignment of union work was bad enough, but what if a kid had gotten hurt?

After I had really had a go at those in the wrong, me and the guys were able to enjoy the funny side of it. By the time I told the story to Frank, Shirley and Dolores back at Local 10, we were all able to have a big laugh about the whole thing.

***

Presente

Tuesday, December 16

After a quick bite of lunch-or was it breakfast?- I hustled over to a Labor Relations Committee meeting at the PCMA. And with yesterday's debacle with the boy scouts, I knew we had them over a barrel. At the meeting I took my sweet time telling the bosses off:

"Child dockers! What's next? Five-year-old girls working the cotton mills? Little boys down in coal mines? Maybe their small bodies will help them get into those little spaces."

"Okay Morrow, we get it," one of them said, but I kept on going. By the end of my rap, I easily got them to agree to hire eight union dockers to replace the "babies." The job only needed four, but I was sure the other side didn't want to go to arbitration, let alone the cops.

Immediately after that I brought up the pay shortages. And well, they couldn't exactly fight me over that either. I knew I had leverage, and I intended to get as much out of it as I could. To put it simply, I hit the jackpot on the settlement. The only downside was I'd have a lot of calls to make when I got back to the office.

After the LRC meeting I headed over to Pier 32. John Tilby greeted me warmly. He told me the tractors and jitneys were back from repair and working just fine. He handed me a dated maintenance form he had prepared to make sure this situation wouldn't arise again. He asked me to sell it to Pier Boss Jack Webster, who'd been fighting me every step of the way on the repairs.

I brought the papers to Webster. Of course, he started to protest, but I warned him that if he fought me on this, I knew of a few other repairs I could demand from them. And that might mean– heaven forbid– another stoppage. He quickly signed the paperwork.

Back at the office, once I'd finished informing the aggrieved parties of our victory with the shortages, I got to work on the next steps of the Kim plan. I called two contacts from Berkeley and one at Stanford. Unsurprisingly, both had heard the rumors of a threatened boycott, and wanted to press me for details. I told them I would meet them tomorrow at two to hand out and discuss copies of the wire the union had drafted for President Chun Doo-hwan. I told them to feel free to bring their translators and any other academics who might be interested.

Driving home that night, I mulled over our tactics in the Korean campaign. It struck me as a little hypocritical that we were refusing to handle the arms shipment to the junta, but we were only hitting Chun Doo-hwan with a threat of what we'd do *if* he executed him. Our opponents might try to level this criticism at us.

The sad truth of the matter was, while El Salvador was a hot button issue, your average Americans didn't know anything about Korean politics. If we launched a boycott before the execution, it would be killed before it even began. We'd have no legal standing and no public support. Once Kim was hanged, we hoped the public would become more aware of the brutality of the dictatorship there and we could build a popular base of support. It was tough, but when it comes to fighting for justice, tactics are half the battle.

37

Wednesday, December 17

The morning started with foreboding news. The State Department made a statement reporting "positive developments" in the junta's restructuring. That could only mean one thing: the suspension of aid was going to be lifted soon. It was almost time to batten down the hatches.

I was met with two quick calls in the office. The first was from Paul, who let me know that a messenger was on his way to Local 10 with fifty copies of the statements on Kim.

"Since we hope our invite captures the tone of our events, I thought I'd read it to you for your approval," Paul quipped with his usual verve.

I snorted, "That's darned funny."

"I figured you might think so."

The next was from Frank, letting me know he was meeting with Tom Augustine and Father McGinnis to discuss the blessing, tentatively scheduled for December 22, and did I want to stop by. Things were pretty quiet in the office, so once Paul's messenger gave me the copies of our statement, I took off.

I arrived at the Archdiocese parking lot just after nine. It's a good thing I did, because there were only two or three spaces left. It was going to be a bigger meeting than just Frank, Tom and Father McGinnis.

As I got out, an old pal spotted me and waved. It was brother John Gurley. John was the first Dominican I'd ever met. Maybe he was also a monk. Whatever religious persuasion he practiced, he taught at a school and worked at what he called a retreat in the hills in the South Bay, near San Jose.

Here was a guy with a big frame and generous manner, vigorous and full of good humor, who'd been born a month after me to a steel-working family in Chi-town. He loved to talk, loved to laugh, and loved to argue. Aside from the collar and cross, he was always dressed like he was about to go camping.

After I parked, we shook hands. "We meet again, mi amigo," he greeted me.

Walking into the Archdiocese, John asked me what the racial climate up at Tara Hills was like, which made me wonder if Susan would be at the meeting.

I shrugged, telling him that the cross burning had stopped and so had the midnight target practice, so perhaps things were back to normal.

He replied (wisely, I thought): "Things have cooled to their usual simmer." We shared our usual cynical chuckle.

John spotted a pair of nuns getting out of their car. It turned out, one of them was Sister Catherine Anne, whom I had met at Tom's meeting when I first announced the aid. She was still dressed like a backpacker, with her Levis and rucksack. With her was Sister Mary Margaret, a bubbly grandmotherly nun I knew from Father McGinnis's staff. She was nearly seventy, and the sight of her, for reasons I didn't fully understand, brought on flashes of old memories and deep feelings from my childhood.

We smiled and said good morning to the women. Right as we did so, yet another car pulled up. How many people could there be at this meeting? When we saw who was in the car, though, we all fell silent.

A teenage boy jumped out of the driver's seat and opened the door for his passenger. A tall, gaunt man with an imposing bearing struggled his way out of the car. He offered us a faint trace of a smile that looked like it required physical effort.

The man was Rabbi Herman Schwartz of Temple Emanu-El, a survivor of the Holocaust and a host of other cruelties before and since. He had a narrow face, shaved close, and wore glasses with wire frames. His brows were shaggy. His eyes dark brown and very clear, open, knowing, and wise. He had a full head of silver-and-black hair, neatly trimmed. As I took in these details, I noted his black raincoat, furled cane-handled black umbrella, dark gray pinstripe suit, vest crossed by a gold watch chain, stiff white high-collared shirt, and tie of muted color. He commanded a real presence.

"Sister Catherine Anne, this is Rabbi Schwartz," the warm Sister Margaret said.

"I am honored to meet you," Schwartz greeted her, barely audible.

"The two of you would have a lot to discuss," Margaret continued, "if Catherine and I might meet in your wonderful study sometime, over a cup of your excellent tea."

The rabbi took a long time to speak, but said: "I would like that. Very much."

Once this group of multidenominational religious figures had assembled, we all made our way into Tom's office. We immediately were met with a traffic jam. It really was a mighty swarm of folks who had turned out. I waded my way through looking for Paul. Instead, I found Tom. After a brief greeting, he gave me the news I'd been anticipating all day: because the junta was being "reorganized," the US economic aid had been resumed.

After a long silence while everyone took in the news, the meeting started. Two minutes into the discussion I got a beep from Mike Garvey. Going out to find a phone, I heard from Mike about a story in tomorrow's *LA Times* saying the suspension had been nothing but a sham in the first place. The article would report that the military pipeline of aid approved prior to October 1st, 1980 (the start of the fiscal year) hadn't been affected at all by the so-called "suspension." It had continued to ship as normal. Nor had any economic aid been halted, except for what had been authorized in fiscal year 1981.

"I hope that helps," Mike said when he had concluded his tip.

"It sure as heck does."

Unfortunately, I had to leave the committee meeting early to get to the meeting I had organized with the academics to discuss Kim. The "leak meeting." Rather than go back in to interrupt only to head out twenty minutes later, I decided to head off early to the leak meeting.

This turned out to be a good call, as the traffic on the way was hellish. What's more, I had to stop off at the Western Union on Ellis to send out the union's wire on Korea. But when I got to Ellis I found the parking situation was even worse than the traffic. How could there be so many cars on the road *and* so many cars *off* the road?

Anyway, I finally found a garage with a vacancy sign and strolled over to Western Union. Here I finally hit some good luck: the counter guy, when he saw what I'd written in the SENDER box, said he thought the longshore union was awesome. I showed him the union's wire, and he said he didn't know about Kim, but definitely knew how bad things were in the ROK.

He gave me stellar service once he saw I was a union man, typing up my confirmation and receipt with lightning speed (even though he typed hunt-and-peck style) and giving me several extra copies of the wire for free. I wished him a happy holidays and got back on the road.

After another bout with the hectic gift-shopper traffic, I got to my next meeting just on time. My contacts at Berkeley and Stanford had certainly spread the word, and there was a group of about fifteen academics waiting for me in Roger's office. I passed each of them a copy of our wire confirmation and receipt and started talking as they scanned the contents.

"Ladies and gentlemen, I'm going to cut right to the chase. I'm sure many of you have heard the rumor circulating about what the union will do if Kim is executed. As you will see in that wire, which I sent less than an hour ago, we are indeed threatening very severe consequences. If the sentence imposed on Kim is carried out, we will pursue with our allies in the Pacific Trade Union Forum the most effective means of protesting that sentence and the rule of Chun Doo-hwan."

I continued by inquiring whether they promised to keep what I tell them top secret. They all restively nodded. I gave them the details of our plan. At ten a.m. the following Monday, after nine months of planning and organizational work we would announce our refusal to load weapons of war for the El Salvador junta. This statement caused quite a stir, but I pushed through. I told them about the second event, the blessing, and how at these events we intended to announce our boycott threat to the ROK government.

"By making this threat in tandem with a much more definite refusal, it will show the Korean government we mean business and help spread the word on the Korean political situation to Americans."

As I concluded my announcement, the academics responded in a way I never would have expected. They started a chant of "Union! Strike! Union! Strike!" Well, I'll be damned if it didn't put a smile on my face.

After that meeting, I headed back to the office to get some of my work done. Once there, Dolores hit me with some sobering info: two old-timers had passed away. I arranged all the info and forms the families would need to benefit from our pension fund, hoping it could be of some help to them in this awful time. I then called the families to say what I always felt was impossible to say. They thanked me and the union and said it would be best if we mailed them the paperwork.

I made my way back home in a somber humor. But then I got a call that lifted my spirits immensely.

"Steve! After all this talk, when are you finally going to let me come along for a day with you?"

It was Susan, her lilt immediately recognizable over the phone. I smirked.

"Alright kid. How does ten o'clock tomorrow at the Local sound?"

I went to bed that night excited for the morning to come.

38

Thursday, December 18

It was Local 10's Election Day for officers, so I headed in early to vote. There were a lot of night folks placing their ballots before heading home for the day, but I didn't mind the long lines. As a matter of fact, it warmed my heart to see everyone turning out to make their voices heard in the union.

Normally an election would be guaranteed to be the biggest event of my day. But with everything going on this year, it felt like that wasn't to be the case.

I got back to my office and made a call to Doug Martin. I let him know about Susan Vogel, and that the two of us would be headed his way over at Pier 50.

"Sure thing, Steve. The dock wouldn't normally be my idea of a date spot, but whatever floats your boat."

"Ha-ha. You're a comedian, you know that? Anyway, me and Susan–"

"Did I hear my name?"

I looked up and there she was, fitted out in a shirt and pants, a safari jacket, hiking boots, a black crush hat, and red bandana popping from her neck.

"How do I look?"

She sure knew how to take my advice about functional gear and make it stylish. I told Doug I'd talk to him later and hung up.

"That'll definitely work," I said, trying to sound nonchalant.

She may have made quite an entrance, but once Susan sat

down it was all business. She told me Tom and Harold had given her a summary of how the strike proceedings would go:

"Let me double-check with you. If the shipment isn't cancelled after the refusal is announced, the PCMA takes you to arbitration. If you don't reach a settlement, then it goes to the courts. Then the judge could force you to load by levying fines."

"Yes, so the only way to avoid eventually loading the cargo is…"

"Public support."

Well, I was impressed. She had saved me a lot of time.

Since she was up to date on the aid situation, I decided to brief her on my old pal Doug Martin, and the goofy terminal boss she'd also meet at Pier 50, Michael McSweeney. I knew the terminal bosses wouldn't be thrilled at the idea of Susan poking her media head around, so I explained that her cover story for McSweeney would be that she's investigating health and safety issues for OSHA.

"Interesting cover. Any reason?"

With that, I told her all about the "powder room" situation over on Pier 50 and how I'd used that to take a look at the shipment. The story made her bowl over laughing.

"Do you often do such things?"

"Well, truth to tell, all the time."

"So, it's really a part of your job?"

"And part of the struggle. Honestly, to me it's the easiest part."

"Well I hope to see some of it firsthand."

We were about to head out to Doug's when Dolores buzzed to say she had a call on hold for me, a reporter from Channel 5 news, the CBS local station. With Susan listening and taking notes, I told Dolores to transfer the call.

"Brother Morrow?"

"Sure is."

"This is Marilyn Spencer. I've heard we might have a story on our hands."

This was a very delicate situation. Almost a dance or a game of chess. I couldn't give Marilyn what I had until I knew what *she* had.

"Is that a fact?" was my opening move.

"It is. And given your history with the Pinochet regime, I had a hunch it might have something to do with El Salvador," she answered.

"Is that all it is? A hunch?"

"Well, maybe a little more than a hunch. And if I'm right, I've got some dope you might want to know."

"Well, whether you're right or not, I'd like to know the dope."

She chuckled.

"Touché, touché. Well, first of all, I happen to know *60 Minutes* is running a piece on El Salvador on Sunday night. That's CBS nationwide. And since it's been in the can a week, they might just tack a news bite onto it. So, if you're going to make news on that front, you might want to tip them off."

I knew this could be an incredible break. But we had to play our cards just right. I got Spencer's number and promised to call her back, then got onto Paul right away. He said he'd set up a conference call with all the heavy hitters and we could make a plan. I told him I'd be available on Doug's phone on Pier 50 in thirty minutes max.

When I asked Susan if she was ready to go, she gave me a wry smile and said: "First let me use the powder room. I hear they've been having some trouble with theirs."

39

On the way to Pier 50, Susan and I drove past the legendary Red's. I told her about the two ginger brothers who ran it, both named "Red," and mentioned that they had the best hot dogs in town.

"Tell you what," she said. "Stop on our way back, I'll treat you to a couple of dogs."

I chuckled and said, "Hey, you're on."

Doug Martin greeted Susan with a wave and a big smile. "Welcome aboard," he said, opening her door. He informed me that McSweeney was out for a while. To me this was good news, but Susan seemed a little disappointed she wouldn't get to try out her cover story.

"I kind of liked being a spy. Especially a toilet spy."

I watched as she quietly slipped out of the office, camera in hand, and walked out onto the pier, her slim figure in silhouette against the ship docked there and the bay beyond.

I used the time to check back in with Paul. He told me he'd made a plan that had already gotten the go-ahead from Pete, Joe, and the rest of the International's Brain Trust.

"Shoot."

The plan was to tell Spencer that we would in fact be speaking about El Salvador, but to be coy on details, instead focusing on the level of support we'd gotten from religious organizations. We wouldn't say any more until we were speaking to a *60 Minutes* crew. If the *60 Minutes* people wanted to talk, we'd tell them we'd refuse to load any weapons of war destined for the junta, but refuse to provide any details on the weapons until our Monday announcement. That way we could hopefully get a lot more coverage for our own media event.

When it came to the *60 Minutes* segment, we wanted a live, five-minute news "bite" at the end of the show interviewing two of our folks in a Channel 5 studio in San Fran.

"I'm leaning toward Tom and myself," Paul added with a chuckle.

I told Paul I heard all that loud and clear. We said our goodbyes and I dialed Spencer's number immediately.

"Spencer here."

"This is Morrow. As to El Salvador, the answer is yes."

"Oh, Jesus. Okay, I've got it. I know it's almost four o'clock back in New York and, with happy hour starting at three, I doubt I'll be able to reach 'Mister Big.' but I'll try to get the producer to tell him what you said. Okay?"

Marilyn said she'd beep me when she had more. I wanted to get out of there before McSweeney came back, but Susan wanted snaps of the cargo, so I kept an eye out for the terminal boss or any other stooges as she slipped into the shed, camera in hand. I loved watching her go in. Not a hint of fear.

By ten after one Susan was back at my side, grinning ear to ear with the snaps she had gotten. Because the terminal boss's car was still not in his slot, I told Susan I'd give him a ring from Red's and say we'd waited over three hours for him. I'd add that his not calling me to say he'd be out could really be bad for business!

She smiled. "Another part of the struggle, right?"

"Hey, it's the easiest part."

***

At a window table in Red's Java House, Susan and I ate our dogs and soaked in the view. A dark sky with a low overcast, the mist wafting between the vast array of cargo ships passing in the harbor.

"I took your advice," she said.

"Oh really? And what, might I ask, was that?"

"I booked another flight for Christmas Eve. Three, in fact. And one on Christmas morning."

"Well, you've certainly got your bases covered."

"Don't worry though, I got a return for the twenty-eighth. You won't get rid of me that easily."

She took a bite of her dog. "What about you? What are your plans for Christmas?"

Something about the way she talked, with her mouth still a little full but her hand covering her lips made me smile.

"Well, to tell the truth, I just haven't thought about them. But I assume that I'll drop in at Paul's and at Frank's, and this year, I'll also stop in at Tom's."

"You don't have a family?"

"Uh-uh."

"At all?"

"Well, not anymore. I mean, I got hitched back in seventy-three. But in November of seventy-eight, I lost my wife in an auto accident."

Susan froze, her eyes wide.

"It was a stormy night, with lots of rain. She was driving home from work when her car got hit by a tractor-trailer out on 101."

"Jesus, Steve. I'm sorry. And you had no children?"

"Right. I mean, I thought we were just starting out. But folks have been really supportive. Most days these past few months, I've been doing okay. The union work helps. I guess you could say it's part of my therapy."

Susan noodled with her straw for a moment.

"As for that, can I ask a personal question?"

I shrugged. "Sure."

"Well, I was going to pry."

"Be my guest, pry away."

"Well, I mean… as part of this 'therapy,' I'd imagine you've got some lady friends."

I hesitated, remembering the promise I had made myself.

"Well… let's just say the 'therapy' has been casual, on a day-to-day basis."

She quit the game.

"I'm sorry you lost your wife, and I'm sorry I brought you back to it."

Despite her words, I could see the smile on her face when she heard I was unattached. I had no idea what to say next, knowing every move was very delicate. You could have cut the tension with a knife.

Luckily for me, at that moment I got a beep. It turned out to be the beep I was waiting on, from Spencer. The producer in New York, a man named Davidson, would be at his desk at a quarter to three. It was now ten after two. Susan and I thanked the waiter and hit the road.

40

"Steve! Marilyn's told me a little about your situation, and even from that I'm excited!"

It was Davidson, the TV producer. I had just gotten through to him from the Local 34 offices, after being put through to two different CBS switchboards and speaking to about five different secretaries.

"So, what do you have for me?" he said.

I told him that we'd announce our refusal to load weapons of war for the junta but would disclose no details prior to our own media event. Suddenly his tone changed.

"Jesus. So how do we get the story?"

"You get it with what I just said."

"But what details can you give me?"

"You get those on Monday with everyone else."

"Come on Steve, you've got to give me *something*."

"Yeah, well, we're talking about a five-minute feed which, as a breaking story, would run at the end of your Sunday program."

"So what? Edit five minutes out of the show we've already recorded and just *give* them to you, carte blanche? With no comment or analysis from our team?"

"Six minutes. You'll need time to introduce us and transfer over to the Channel 5 studio."

"Jesus. Look, if it emerges that we should talk more, I'll let you know through Spencer."

"Okay."

The call ended in a draw.

"Well, that was blunt," Susan remarked.

I told her we should go to the union's photo shop to get her prints developed before the planning meeting tonight. As she was gathering her things, I received a call from Reverend Roger Morris. He told me he had just been at a meeting with a group of Korean students and academics. They had just read Frank's defense of Kim and damning of Doo-hwan and wanted to send their thanks to the union. Because of our wire and what one man had described as "the union's most noble past," they all were hopeful that Kim wouldn't be executed.

Well that just made me well up with emotion. I thanked Roger for passing on the kind words and promised I'd tell Frank, Paul and the rest of the guys.

After dropping off Susan's film, we went to a café next door to write notes and recall the day, which Susan said was "wonderfully real and exciting." We ordered a tea and a joe and, somewhat embarrassingly, split a tuna on rye.

***

We spent that evening in the war room (the office at Local 10) with the rest of the core planning committee for El Salvador. Just a sea of weary, hungry comrades eating Chinese take-out and discussing battle maneuvers. There are worse ways to spend an evening.

"That man's a goddamn menace," Frank had joked as he shook Susan's hand. I noticed how much all the guys seemed to enjoy the company of Susan Vogel. Like me, they were quite taken with her, staying quite polite and soft-spoken whenever they addressed her. For Susan's part, she nodded, smiled, and laughed along with the union boys when funny or goofy things were brought up. She was clearly getting a kick out of their stuff.

At seven-forty I got a beep and excused myself from the meeting. Sure enough, it was Marilyn from CBS. I called and asked her what the good word was.

"Well, I'm not in the loop, so I don't know what they want to talk about, but I just gave your number to a switchboard gal in NYC. Mister Big, a guy named Rowe, will call you in fifteen minutes. You'll need another code."

"Hold on a sec." I had left my pen in the meeting room and went fumbling around the desk for another. When I got one, I said: "Okay, you may fire when ready, Gridley."

"Jesus Morrow, you would try the patience of Job."

"Hey! Now that's a good line."

She gave me the code, which again was about thirty digits. Before calling it back to her I said: "Jesus, Spencer, you would try the patience of Job."

Not even a chuckle.

After going through the same lengthy process as before, eventually I got through to Mr. Big.

"Mister Morrow?"

"Speaking."

"As I'm sure you know, this is Norman Rowe. I'm calling because I—and an office full of my best technical people at Channel 5—would like to start getting more details. Can you meet with my folks at Channel 5 at nine your time?"

"I'll be there."

"Amazing. We can talk more once you're there."

As I went back to the lobby, I saw Susan coming down the stairs with a smile and an escort of five stewards. I told Susan the news and asked if she wanted to come to Channel 5 with me or call it a night.

"I'm with you as far as this thing goes, Steve."

"All right then." I asked the stewards to fill Frank in on the developments and headed out to the van.

Over at Channel 5 they were already expecting me, and they led us straight to the office of a technical team. While we waited for Big's call, our hosts rapped about how they wanted what they called "the Pulitzer shots," saying they wanted the piece to have "the look of *On The Waterfront.*"

Then Rowe got on the line and took charge. He gave a rundown of their ideas for the visuals of the piece, complete with settings, scenes, and descriptions of camera angles. After a half hour of this, he asked me what I thought. Because he had focused on the visuals, I got the sense he was trying to butter me up. I repeated what I'd said to Davidson earlier: we wanted a five-minute feed of a breaking news story at the end of *60 Minutes.*

He sighed and answered, "Gimme a second," then put us on hold. A few minutes later he was back.

"Mister Morrow. We've had a chat about what to do with your five. We were thinking, why not longer for you and, at least, a little for us? We first thought to give you six or seven minutes, with one or two minutes of commentary afterwards. But let me cut right to the chase—how about twenty for you, ten for us? We could start shooting tonight. We could even do a whole breaking news program."

He paused. When I said zip, he went back to jive.

"We're talking an offer you can't refuse here."

I stayed cool.

"I'll pass it on," I said. My response seemed to surprise Rowe, like he expected me to jump up and down in excitement.

"Okay, sure. But what do think?"

"Look. I'll pass it on to my leaders and, when it's my turn, I'll get to that."

He sighed. "Fine. When do you think we'll hear?"

"I'll call Channel 5 when there's something to say."

"Okay. But just to confirm: the offer you made to Davidson is still on the table, right?"

"Well, until I pass on your current offer."

"Wait. Are you saying our new offer might somehow threaten things?"

"Well, folks could get skittish."

"Jesus. So, maybe it would be best to go back to that."

"That's up to you."

There was another pause.

"Look, pass on what I have just said now, and when we want to talk again, Channel 5 will call you."

When we had hung up, I asked for an office with desk and a phone. Arrangements were made, and I was shortly on the phone to Paul. I reported what had happened, and he said he'd schedule a conference call with his squad and Frank and Tom for seven tomorrow morning.

I also got some of the results from the elections. Brother Curtice and Brother Wright had been elected full-time Business Agents, which I was happy to hear. Paul asked me to brief them on the aid shipment and on Kim. We shared an enthusiastic "Right on!" as we signed off.

Driving back to Tom's lot, Susan summarized the day as being "terribly real." I told her I'd pick her up in the same place at six the next morning.

"Well," she said as we pulled up, "thanks for an exciting first day."

She got out, walked over to her rental and drove off into the night. I hung around for a minute after she was gone. Then I went home and fixed myself a drink.

41

Friday, December 19

The day began with an ominous full circle moment when Nick Rowan, whose call from Pier 50 on December 3rd launched this entire escapade, called me up. He informed me that the *Tropic Wind*, being trailed by a tug, had just steamed by heading to her berth.

It was here.

I thanked Nick and told him I was sorry not to have kept in touch. I was embarrassed, and said as much.

"No worries, Steve, I know you're out there watching the game."

I told him the stewards and I would be at the Tick Tock at noon if he wanted to join us. He signed off by joking that come dispatch he'd try to "catch the wind."

I got moving and picked up Susan at six on the dot over at the Archdiocese lot, pleased she was right on time. As we clattered across the Third Street Bridge it dawned on me: with the *Wind* docked at Pier 50, we could no doubt see it from Local 34 just down the street.

We drove through light traffic, moving parallel to a narrow inlet as it opened out into the wider Mission Bay, and pulled into 34. The view ahead of us looked like a picture from a painting: the *Wind* was aglow, framed by the dotted lights of the buildings downtown against a still, nocturnal backdrop.

"A scene of great promise and risk," Susan said, sitting next to me.

Once she took a few snaps of the ship, we headed over to the Tick Tock. We sat with a bunch of our folks who had already claimed a corner table and broke our fast: she with French toast and OJ, and I with scrambled eggs, bacon and toast.

We caught up with the guys, who were complaining about how clueless and out of touch that morning's news was. I felt an air of mounting tension in the room; the kind you feel before a big fight.

As Doug Martin got up to leave, he lifted his coffee mug and made a toast: "As for the aid to the junta, here's to moving nothing, solidarity with the people of El Salvador!"

The rest of the guys met that with a big cheer. At that moment I got a beep.

It was Channel 5, Rowe wanted to talk. I drove back to my local with Susan, where I called Channel 5 back. Rowe was giving me more jive about all the shots they wanted to get and inviting me over to Channel 5 for "a hearty breakfast." I don't know why, but something about it struck me as off. I told them I'd see what I could do and got off the line.

I called Paul to give him my updates on the Channel 5 situation. Paul had no news. I called Frank, who was working on what was sure to be one of the most memorable bulletins in the union's history. He said he had only started to block things out but was considering a title, in caps: AS FOR THIS DAY—HISTORIC.

I told him it was dynamite. Along with that bulletin, Frank would also have a half-sheet throwaway for the day and night dispatches on both Sunday and Monday titled "A DAY YOU'LL REMEMBER." This flyer would advise that on that day, the Monday of Christmas Week, our union would hold a press conference to make an historic announcement.

With that, Frank laughed and said a "customer" was coming in, and he'd be in touch.

With the uneasy feeling in my stomach about the news piece,

I decided to give a call to my reliable reporter pal Jim Birch, who I figured would know the inside track.

Jim answered with a growl, "Yeah?"

I replied that I was calling, as promised, but it was nice to hear his cheery voice.

"Alright," he responded in a still-sour voice. But when I said I wanted his thoughts on some probing and fooling around by the CBS folks in New York, he came quickly to life.

"Sure! Anything I can do," he said with fresh enthusiasm. I filled him in on the whole scenario, and he was ready with his take.

"My guess is that they're in real trouble. All they've got in the can right now is a puff piece, bad reporting. Now with arms involved and your invite, they know your news is gonna be big. Now, big is good, but not when it makes them look bad. If they just run 5-minutes with you at the end of their already-planned show, that will expose their piece as fluff.

"So, somebody in New York is saying 'cancel the Sunday junk, build a new piece on this news.' Except here's the big problem: the union's action will challenge the Reaganites who already are in power when it comes to El Salvador. So CBS might have to choose between going with the dockers and religious folks and featuring a big headline story, or staying friendly to Reagan by burying this story."

All that made perfect sense to me. I thanked Jim profusely for helping me understand the game. Susan agreed that his argument was "very persuasive indeed."

Now all we had to do was wait for the next New York call.

We walked along the esplanade to the Tick Tock. The dockers and stewards for the *Wind* were all meeting for lunch, so I asked Susan if she'd like to go in and meet them. She said "in a second" and started taking pictures of the old greasy spoon. Its neon sign, the parking lot, the truckers hanging around shooting the breeze. It meant a lot to me that she could see how important this place was, see it as more than just some diner, as the sight of a lot of history and emotion.

Susan might have noticed some look on my face betraying my thoughts, because she told me she'd make copies of the pictures for me. With that, we headed inside and joined the guys. I was pleased to find that Nick Rowan, who had first spotted the arms on the dock, had decided to join the group. I shook his hand and thanked him for his work. Then Doug Martin, who seemed prone to sentiment today, raised his cup and said: "This lunch is on me, Nick. It's an honor to have you here."

In the middle of food, I got another beep. Given the time, I thought it would be about Kim, but it turned out to be from Rowe. I called him back, but after getting the tip from Jim I was sure to keep up my firm defense.

"Great news, Steve! We just managed to confirm Dan Rather, a lead anchor for *60 Minutes*, to do your piece. He can fly out to San Francisco and be at Channel 5 to handle the interviews in person."

He waited for a response. I just said, "So we've got your final offer?"

"Ha!" he snorted. "What more could there be?"

"I'll pass it on."

"So, maybe in an hour or so?"

"Yeah. Maybe."

I hung up and called Paul right away. I filled him in on Jim's take and my last call with Rowe. Paul thanked me and said he'd have to take all this into consideration. Two minutes after our phone call ended, he beeped me again. I called him back.

"Steve. I know a trap when I see one. It's a no."

Paul went on to say that our previous offer, what we'd suggested right off the bat, was still on the table.

Susan was shocked when I told her the news. We went to dial

CBS right away, but at that moment I got *another* beep. It was the one I'd expected earlier from The Reverend Roger Morris. When he answered the phone he was close to tears.

"Steve, it's– can you believe it? He…he *hasn't been hanged*! Kim hasn't been hanged!"

He was right. I couldn't believe it.

"What? How? *Why?*"

Roger said he had no explanation, but it had been announced by the ROK. For now, at least, it was true.

"There's a lot to do here, Steve, I just wanted to make sure you knew. I'll be in touch as soon as we know more."

"Thanks, brother."

I walked back to the table to pass on the news, when I was met with a group of people already celebrating. I asked what had happened, and Doug told me that he, too, had gotten a beep.

He said that all the gangs would finish their work by three forty-five, and the *Wind* would sail at four. When I opened my mouth to object, Doug assured me they weren't ordered to load any military cargo. I said that was amazing and told the guys about Kim, which made them even happier.

Susan took a sip of her tea and showed her pearly whites: "Well, Steve. At least for today, all's well with the world."

I decided not to rain on her parade by pointing out that the weapons were still on the dock and the government still hadn't backed down. Instead, I smiled back and saluted her, clicking her glass of tea with my coffee cup.

I sure wanted to kiss the hand holding that cup of tea.

42

After a jovial lunch, Susan and I headed back to the office, where I put through a call to CBS. They said Rowe wasn't available right now, and I said that was fine and to let him know we were saying no to his offer. Hanging up, I was pretty sure Rowe would become "free" very shortly.

Soon after that I got more word from Roger. The latest was that Kim had received a kind of stay and had been returned to his prison cell.

"All of us here are very positive, but we're not quite ready to celebrate."

Then we got the anticipated Rowe call. I listened to him bark a lot of phrases like "Christ Almighty" and "I'll be a God-damned son of a bitch." Clearly, they had assumed the ILWU would jump at their "generous" offer.

I replied that our original offer still was there: 5 minutes at the conclusion of their already-planned episode. He grumbled that he'd call me tomorrow.

"Well, what now?" Susan asked with open curiosity.

"Now, even on a day like today, I have to do my regular work. We can't turn all this diverted attention into an opportunity for workers to get even more screwed over."

I spent the next few hours sorting out a dispute over in Local 29 about a promised new computer network. It was pretty tough going, but by the end of things I was feeling pretty optimistic about the outcome. It seemed like nothing could go wrong today.

And then I got a call from Doug, who said he was relieved he caught me at the office.

"It's bad news, Steve."

Apparently, the guys working the *Wind* had all been put on standby to work "a now anticipated release of additional cargo." We were back to square one: they might be asked to load the aid tonight.

Tonight? That gave the union only a matter of hours to get a wildcat started, *and* notifying our friends in the Archdiocese, not to mention the press, other unions, other church groups…

I told him I'd drive over to Local 34 immediately and set up shop there, so I'd be close by in case it was go time. Susan and I got in the rig and speeded across town. Once I'd been set up with a desk and phone, I called Paul, Frank and Tom, all in quick succession. Everyone was in dismay: we all thought there would be a brief moment of safety in this bitter fight, and now the war could be starting even sooner than we thought.

In the middle of this frenzy, I got another beep from Reverend Morris. Tom insisted I take it, and we said our goodbyes.

It now seemed that Kim, for unknown reasons, would be granted the right to appeal to the Supreme Court. Roger continued, laughing: "That party I was joking that it's too soon for earlier? Well, we're actually having it. A student named Young Chu has been given the much-coveted honor of asking you to join them."

Roger passed the phone and a squeaky, excited voice took over.

"Hello, hello, Mister Steve?"

"Yes, speaking."

"Thank you! Kim has been saved! Sometimes, the people win. Your union wire was very important. Yes, very important. People are very grateful."

I smiled. "The execution is called off? Well, that's wonderful news."

"Yes, yes. And our deep thanks from all the Korean people."

He seemed to choke up, then added, "If the situation with the Salvadoran aid is okay, please come to our wonderful celebration."

I apologized and explained that I couldn't get there, at least not right away. But, I assured him, everyone in the union would celebrate this victory right along with them.

As I got off the line I realized that I, too, was welling up. And so it shouldn't have surprised me when I looked up and saw that Susan was starting to cry.

"I'm sorry," she said, "I just need to go to the Ladies Room."

She was back after about five minutes, offering me a faint smile.

"One thing you should know about me, Steve. I sometimes cry when the news is bad. But I *always* cry when the news is good."

Even as she said that, I felt she was one tough cookie, because once she'd had her cry she got her traction back. She suggested that we should probably have a bite now, while we could. "You can't go into battle on an empty stomach, now can you?"

"I guess not," I said. "But we'll have to make it fast, there's a ship's cargo of work to be done."

We pulled up to Blanche's Galleria, a rambling old wood shack at the southwest end of the Fourth Street Bridge. The reason I suggested going there– besides it being near the *Wind*–was that a lot of dockers had gone there in the distant past. Back then it was called Crabby John's. Always on Friday at noon, when we were working nearby at the dock where we unloaded bananas from Central America, we ordered the same treat: a crab salad on a French roll. To any old-timer on the waterfront, it was still Crabby John's.

Nowadays though, things had changed. The dockers were gone–their old haunt had been gentrified for the business-world clientele that had set up in that neighborhood. They didn't even serve the crab salad anymore. But any time I passed there, I was flooded with a thousand memories and stories from the good old days. That must have been what made me think of it now, as I was living out another story.

I told Susan most of that before we arrived. She seemed touched by the whole thing and thanked me for bringing her there. We arrived and were seated at a corner table for two, a shielded orange candlelight between the two of us. We ordered cold cuts and cheeses, quiche with mushrooms and sausage, and raw veggies with two different dips. It certainly wasn't the old days, but I've got to admit, it was tasty.

We lifted our glasses–a seltzer with lime for Susan, a Dos Equis Amber for me, and said, "Cheers." Digging into our food and reviewing the day together, it occurred to me that I hadn't had a meal this nice since my wife died.

"I'm glad we came out here, Susan," I confessed.

"So am I, Steve," she said, smiling into her glass.

And right at that moment, darned if I didn't get a beep. Susan said she'd pay the tab and I should get to a phone out front. I did and soon heard from Doug. Howard and Hank's gangs had been released, while Harvey's and Axel's gangs would remain on standby.

"Damn," I said. "Is this it?"

"Wait, there's more." Doug told me he'd found out that earlier the Tropic Steamship Line, the company that owned the *Tropic Wind*, had been asked by the consulate staff of El Salvador to delay her departure so it could load an expensive shipment of New Year's booze, beer, and wine meant for what the consulate said were wealthy Salvadorans.

"Wait. You mean the 'additional cargo'…"

"Is booze!"

"And the *Wind* isn't shipping out tonight?

"Not a snowball's chance," said Doug.

With the stress that had been building up all day, I couldn't help but burst into laughter. Everyone I called (thank the gods I still had some dimes in my pocket), from Frank to Jim Birch, had the same response. It was really just beyond belief, a darned good tale. Then I called Paul to pass on the news.

"I'll be damned" was all he said. He didn't laugh.

"What's the matter, brother?"

"Let's talk later. I'll set up a call for tonight."

In truth, I really wanted to get back in gear while having a drink on my couch, so I was glad when Susan asked me to drop her at her car.

"What do you think Paul wants to talk about?" she asked in the car. I explained to her that although the booking had been cancelled for the *Wind*, the aid could be drayed to the Oakland Army Base and then sent to El Salvador via Panama.

"Just like the shipments to Chile in seventy-eight," she said.

I turned to my passenger with an expression of utter shock. "Yes… exactly like that."

She laughed heartily. "I'm interested in your field, Steve, remember?"

I recovered and went on that if the shipping was rebooked for the *Moon* and loaded on an army base, we'd have to follow a trailer to see where it ended up. There might even be a stakeout.

We pulled into Tom's parking lot and I turned the engine off. She didn't get out of the car right away. Instead, she just looked at me.

"Good night," I said.

"Good night, Steve," she said, still not getting out. She put her hand by the gear shift, almost touching mine. I lifted my hand up and, for a moment, thought about putting it over hers. But then I moved it back across my lap.

"I'll call you tomorrow," I said.

After a brief pause, Susan smiled and nodded, then opened the door. I waited for her to pull out, then waved. I was glad we hadn't touched hands, knowing only just too well what that would have done to my feelings. Like I'd told her at lunch the other day, I was doing better since the death of my wife, and part of that doing better was keeping things casual. But as she drove away, I realized that what I was feeling for Susan was far from casual, and I didn't know if I could handle it.

43

As I got in that night and poured myself a drink, I received my latest beep from Doug. I called and he gave me an update on the *Wind*:

"In the end, the Salvadorans decided to send their booze entirely by air. So the extra crews were not needed."

"Oh well," I joked, "The men got paid for less work, that's never a bad thing."

"It's not all good news, Steve. I got an update from GHQ."

Doug reported that the Sharpe Depot had canceled the booking, but the Department of Defense had confirmed the authorization of the shipment. As a result, starting at eight o'clock tomorrow morning, three trailers would be hauled to Pier 32 by three tractor drivers, who would each make six trips, and each driver would have two helpers, to assist in setting up a locked corral of chain-link fence for every three trailers.

Doug said that both he and the Chief Clerk of 50 had received new orders. So, Doug would return the paperwork on the aid to the chief in the morning, and then to the Sharpe Depot. Although none of the paperwork for trailers would specify its freight, it would give its total weight, and the chief would issue an order of transit for each trailer. When the receiving clerk had countersigned that order, the drivers would return all the paperwork to him.

I thanked Doug for the dynamite work and asked him to call me as soon as he got to his shack in the morning.

Now, things were still murky to me, to say the least. But when I called Paul and told him the latest from Doug, he came up with a major-league play. He started by saying he just didn't buy into the claim that they held those gangs on overtime just to load booze, even for the biggest of big shots. Even if that explanation was partly true, there must've been something more than booze that could've arrived for loading.

"I don't care what way you shake it. If they transported it by air, the amount of booze involved could *not* have required four gangs to work it."

Paul concluded that the whole darn excuse could have been used as cover for the DOD's rebooking some of the aid to beat the suspension but, when that was finally ruled out, the booking of aid to the *Moon* had been canceled to hide what had been planned. When its paperwork is returned to Sharpe and the cargo was drayed from the dock with only an order of transit, there was no paper trail to or from Pier 50 that someone could trace. And because the folks at Pier 32 would only have the number of each trailer and the weight of its freight, the military aid for the junta that had been loaded and what it consisted of could not be discovered, let alone proved.

It was one slick sleight of hand by the DOD.

Next, Paul outlined our response strategy. First, at the media event we'd simply call the cargo a "shipment of arms." Hopefully this would encourage a response of outright lies and pooh-poohing by the government.

"They don't know that we have documents that prove what's in that shipment," Paul rolled on, "If we don't convey anything in detail, maybe they'll assume we don't have any details."

"We entrap them," I said. It was brilliant.

Paul assigned me the task of drafting an exposé detailing the nature, purpose and trail of the shipment at Pier 32 that we could drop when the moment was finally right.

We ended our call full of excitement. We had a plan that, if the government behaved like we thought they would, might gain us a lot of credibility in the public eye. My immediate instinct was to call up Susan and tell her all about it. But as my hand reached for the phone, I hedged. Instead, I called Frank, who thought Paul's "go-for-broke plan," as he put it, was genius. After a quick chat with my old friend, I went to bed.

For hours, my mind raced with details to be included in the exposé. But eventually, a wave of fatigue crashed over me and washed me away to a deep sleep.

44

I was still lying in bed when I got a call from Marilyn Spencer.

"Is it about the *60 Minutes* piece?" I asked, my voice still groggy, "or do you just like to chat at seven a.m. at the weekend?"

"Rowe's decided to scrap the feature idea. He said the feature we already have has been in the can too long."

"Do you buy that?"

Marilyn's sharp voice paused a moment.

"Don't ask."

After that I called Susan to work out our plans for the day. I didn't mention my exposé assignment, wanting to keep it close to the vest until I knew more. Instead, I told her I'd be very busy this morning doing some "chores."

"What kind of chores?" she asked.

"Oh, you know. Sweep and mop the floors. Wash, dry, and fold my clothes. Check my fridge and make a shopping list for the week. Just things like that."

"Right, right. And you also have that exposé you're working on, I imagine that'll take a lot of time."

I broke out into a smile. The lady was resourceful.

We ended up having a long chat. Work was a part of it, but we also discussed how we normally like to spend our weekends in calmer times. Eventually I really had to get off the phone. We agreed she'd hitch a ride with Tom to the media meeting Tom was having and I'd meet her there if I had time. I hated to hang up the phone.

I got myself a joe and an OJ, sat at my desk and started to think about how best to frame the exposé. That's when I got a call from Tom Augustine. Sounding unusually pressing, he asked me to call Maria Martinez "right away." Maria was our main source on the United Salvadoran Patriotic Forces (or FUPS), the U.S.-based front group allied with the El Salvadoran military junta. I hadn't spoken to Maria since the beginning of this whole journey in early December, but back then I had found her insights about FUPS and the Hernandez brothers extremely helpful. I was excited by any opportunity to speak to her again.

Maria answered the phone and immediately apologized for how long it had taken her to get her information.

"No apology necessary, Miss Martinez. Thank you for the incredible work you're doing."

"Since I spoke to you and Mister Augustine last, my investigations have borne some interesting fruit."

Maria said she had discovered that back in June, Colonel Tomás Hernandez, the named recipient of the aid we were supposed to ship, had bought a warehouse in San Salvador from the National Guard. He paid only 2,000 U.S. dollars for the entire complex.

Hernandez quickly had it secured behind a double-wire fence manned by armed security. He had the warehouse remodeled and renamed it—Maria spelled it out for me—the "Terminal de la Nueva Nación." From then on, every few weeks columns of military trucks delivered freight to the warehouse. From the warehouse, supplies were distributed, sometimes in military trucks and other times by commercial vehicles.

"Do you know what's in the vehicles?" I asked.

"No. We gathered our information from copies of the terminal's paperwork, passed on to us by truck drivers sympathetic to our cause. What we do know is the receipts from the shippers are always marked with the capital letters *I, A, T,* and *G.*" Maria explained that this stood for the Inter-American Trade Group, who were listed in the billing accounts as the shipper of the goods.

"We did some digging, and the Inter-American Trade Group is an organization owned and operated by–"

"Guillermo Hernandez." Maria had explained to me in our last call how Guillermo ran the American side of the wealthy Hernandez family's operations, supporting the FUPS and helping to foster the aggression towards Salvadoran communists in this country.

"Exactly," Maria said. Apparently, Hernandez, using the IATG, had become "the official purchasing agent of all U.S. furnishings and luxury items for the officer class of El Salvador."

So, Guillermo Hernandez ordered and distributed goods on behalf of the junta (including Colonel Hernandez) from his consulate office. The goods were shipped by people who usually shipped goods to hotels and resorts, and was all overseen by the West Coast vice president of Tropic Steam. Unfortunately, Maria still knew very little about the kind of freight involved. I said I'd ask my Pier 50 pal what he knew of IATG and report back any news.

I told Maria I'd be on page all day and said "muchas gracias."

"De nada y adiós."

I knew the IATG connection sounded seedy. But there were still a lot of jigsaw pieces we needed to put into place.

45

I called up Doug, the "Pier 50 pal" I'd mentioned to Maria.

"Steve, I should've known I wouldn't get a lie-in with you on the case. What's going on?"

I laughed and we got into it.

"Well, it's kind of vague, but I just heard of a company that does the buying– but not the packing and shipping– of luxury stuff for the officer corps in El Salvador. Food, booze, other fancy furnishings. It's called the Inter-American Trade Group. Ever heard of 'em?"

"I'll be a son of a bitch," Doug replied. The shipper involved in last night's delay of the *Star* was listed as I-A-T-G."

"That's what I suspected."

"The name only showed up in pier records a few months ago, but since then they've been buying all kinds of stuff that, to put it mildly, would be absolutely out of the reach for most folks in El Salvador."

"Do you know anything about the company?"

"Jesus, not a thing. No matter what they're shipping or who they're shipping with, the paperwork only listed them by their billing code, I-A-T-G."

"In other words, they're shadowy."

"Boy, that's for sure."

Then Doug gave me a list of the items they had shipped over. I couldn't believe my ears. Stoves, refrigerators, dishwashers, washing machines, televisions, stereo systems, hand-crafted cowboy boots and hats, pool tables, full wet bars, and–worst of all–Jacuzzis. This in a country where 90% of the population were suffering from malnutrition. To rub salt in that wound, Doug told me about some of the gourmet foods they were ordering: caviar, conger eel, and even tinned snails!

He told me he could have a comprehensive list over to me by noon. I thanked him and jumped off the line. Next, I was all set to call Paul and give him the latest when my phone rang. It was my lady friend, the one I'd been seeing casually.

"Because there was no headline this morning, you must be moving on to your media event and the blessing?" she said energetically. I didn't want to give her a full update on all the developments, so all I said was, "Yep, that's right."

She went on to tell me that with work kind of slow due to the holidays, she decided to take two weeks' vacation. She had a taxi coming for her at two today, and she'd return on the fourth of January.

It occurred to me that I felt a little relieved when I heard her say that. I felt guilty about it, but I really didn't feel much of a desire to see her with everything that had been going on. I decided to think about all that later, and just said: "Have a nice time. We can go for dinner when you get back."

"Sure thing. And I'll have my eye on the news!"

Finally, I was on the line with Paul. As I suspected, he was outraged to hear about the connections between Guillermo Hernandez, the Tropic Steam Shipping Line and the junta. Still, he wasn't surprised. Tropic Steam had always been a thorn in our side, fighting our union at every turn. They were known for their arrogance and extravagance. When they had first set up a West Coast office in 1976, they had bought a huge penthouse office at One Embarcadero, where their execs could look out at the bay like overlords.

Paul and I agreed that I could play into this arrogance in my exposé, and we agreed that we'd talk more later.

After that, I launched into my exposé. My anger at the morning's developments was serving as an inspiration for me, and I wrote as much from my heart as my head. I got a call from John Tilby to let me know he'd received a drayage request form for Pier 32, just as we'd expected. It didn't specify what cargo was being moved, but we both agreed to keep a close eye on it. Apart from that one interruption, I spent much of the morning unleashing the first draft of my exposé. I knew we weren't releasing it yet, but as I wrote, it felt like I was finally telling the story of these past few weeks to the world.

***

I made ten copies of what I had written, putting nine in my folder on aid, folding the other and putting it in my coat pocket for Susan. Then I swung over to Red's to get the paperwork from Doug. He offered to buy me a beer, but I said I'd have to take a raincheck. I made a quick stop to make copies of Doug's paperwork, which listed every item the IATG had shipped in the last months. That taken care of, I headed over to the International–home base–where Susan and I had agreed to meet.

I stepped into the big conference room, where a big meeting had been going on for a while. I greeted the participants–Paul, Tom Augustine, secretary-treasurer Pete Turner, and about a dozen folks from our media co-ordination team– and apologized for being late. Spotting Susan in the back scribbling studiously in a notebook, I took a seat next to her.

"What'd I miss?" I asked.

"Oh, you didn't hear? The aid's already halfway to El Salvador," she teased me. Susan filled me in on what they had discussed. It was mostly logistics about setting up the equipment and what order the speakers would go up in.

The meeting was just about finishing at that point. When most of the crew had wandered over to the generous deli spread in the back of the hall, Susan and I approached Paul, Tom and Peter. I gave my four companions each a copy of what Doug had given me, and we surveyed them together.

We could hardly believe our eyes.

"This is something else," Pete said.

It would take a week to list all the items these people had shipped. But for starters, they had an alcohol list longer than my whole body, including Macallan and J&B rare whiskey, as well as the finest cognacs and even Drambuie! In a country where many people struggle to access water, these officers felt they needed an after-dinner liqueur.

There was an array of exotic seafood and meat, shipped fresh from Los Angeles with detailed refrigeration instructions. Then the trimmings– pallets of all kinds of sauces and mustards, pickled peppers and artichoke hearts, and all things of that variety.

Finally, we got to the folder marked "Furnishings," which was so big it had to be broken down room by room: Office, Living Room, Dining Room, Master Bedroom, Children's Room, Kitchen, Bath, Rec Room, and Patio. Patio furniture!

After a few moments getting rightly steamed together, we all agreed this was great material to use against the junta and to gain the American public's favor. Tom suggested I call Maria and fill her in on what I had found, which I thought was a great idea.

Luckily, I got through after just a few rings.

"Maria! This is Steve. I'm calling because I wanted to fill you in on 'una cosa más'," which I hoped meant "one more thing."

She asked me for a rundown, and I reported that G. and T. Hernandez were central to the junta's rule because each of them played a vital role in supplying its officer class with the things that come with wealth.

Maria asked what I proposed. I said that on the Tuesday after the union hall blessing ceremony I'd be meeting with representatives from PCMA, the folks on the other side, at their office. As a deterrent to their filing grievances against the union's refusal to handle the arms cargo on Monday, I'd fully detail the aid, how we could prove what it was and think it would be used.

After that meeting, I would set up an off-the-record one—with my contract counterpart in the PCMA, vice president of Tropic Steam, and, with luck, a rep or two of the Department of Defense. As another deterrent, we could pass details of the Hernandez-Tropic connection to the junta, its weapons of war, and the luxury goods provided the officer class on to the press.

These would be the main points: Hernandez and Tropic had seen, early on, the emergence of the Reagan cold war and how that could be good for their bottom line, since instruments of war would become a growth industry. Because of the influence Hernandez had in the Reagan camp, Tropic got a new contract to haul arms to El Salvador.

Maria echoed my words to Paul earlier: "A perfect one-two punch."

I got off the line and returned to the guys. I told Paul that with all the new paperwork, I should make some drastic changes to my exposé piece. Paul agreed, and I said I was going to go home to get right to it.

I turned to Susan to ask if she'd be alright getting back to her car, but she preempted what I was going to say: "I'll be fine, Steve. You go write this thing."

I spent the entire evening holed up at my desk, a take-out box of Mongolian Beef by my side, trying to figure out the best way to lay this whole thing out. Every time I did a draft it felt like I was leaving something essential out, but then when I included every detail the piece lacked punch.

Presente

At around 9 p.m., Susan called to let me know she'd gotten home and to ask how the piece was going. I told her about my troubles making everything short and sweet.

"You'll get there," she reassured me. "There's no one better to write this thing than you."

"Thanks Susan. Maybe I'll see you tomorrow at GHQ?"

I knew as soon as I said this that it couldn't happen. Not with this job hanging over me. Still, it felt good when I heard her say: "Sure thing, Steve. I'll save you a seat."

46

I had a dream that night where Susan and I lay on a beach together in Coos Bay, gazing out at the horizon. When I awoke fragments of it lingered in my foggy head for hours. I needed to take time to sort through what I was feeling, but who had time on pivotal days such as these?

Tom Augustine called me early to invite me to his place that evening for "a glass of wine and light repast to watch *60 Minutes*" with him and his wife, Roberta, and Father McGinnis, Susan, and Paul. I said that sounded terrific and gave Roberta my best. I was darned interested to see how the piece turned out without our input.

I'd barely begun my writing when Maria called with a real humdinger. She reported that the United Salvadoran Patriotic Forces had announced this morning that Señor G. Hernandez will honor Reagan on his inauguration night with a speech titled 'New Reagan World in Our Beloved El Salvador: Freedom, Hope, and Trade,' at a banquet organized by the California Conservative Council. After the speech Herman Reynolds, West Coast head of the Tropic Steamship Line, will thank Señor Hernandez.

Maria punched things home:

"From our sources up here, we now can confirm that the purchasing done by Hernandez is the work of Reynolds and his staff." She closed by telling me that the latest would be in the weekly FUPS newsletter, which they always handed out on Sundays at the steps of the Mission Dolores church. She said she could give me a copy if I called around to the Archdiocese building, where she'd be working late and watching *60 Minutes* with some friends. Before hanging up, we laughed that our Sundays would be filled with more work.

I reported Maria's latest to Paul, who called it "a thoroughly revealing example of the Reaganite-jackboot connection." Paul suggested I really hammer it home in my exposé, saying, "the wealth and luxury goods in contrast to the misery and poverty among the majority of Salvadorans would be front-page news in the *Examiner*."

I agreed that the hardball approach was the way to go and continued with my work. Soon Paul called me back to confirm that Pete Turner, Joe Margolis, Frank Spaulding, Tom and Father McGinnis had all approved of his approach. They had also agreed to "hold back" some of our supporters, meaning those scheduled to speak at the blessing event would be held in reserve for a potential additional event we might need to hold. In other words, we would delay the blessing until after our formal on-the-job refusal.

Paul added that I'd soon receive a copy of the union's official statement of refusal. That statement would include proof that "a substantial shipment of military weapons is now located at Pier 32." It would also point out that despite Carter's "suspension," aid from the previous fiscal year continued to be delivered. The declaration would end with good moral stuff about opposing war and condemning the donation of weapons to authoritarian regimes for use against their own people, and so on. I praised his finely crafted choice of words that were, in my opinion, absolutely terrific.

We went on to discuss who I should send my exposé to. I suggested we deliver copies to Dobbs at the PCMA, Reynolds at the Tropic Steamship Line, and someone at DOD. If I could get Dobbs to read it and arrange a meeting with the PCMA on Tuesday, after the blessing ceremony, I'd speak to the main points, noting each was keyed to one or more folders of proof.

Paul agreed and suggested a killer negotiation tactic. In all of my meetings, I was to indicate that if the aid was officially cancelled and we were confident it would not ship, we would keep quiet about our refusal. However, if we learned that anything about our refusal was made public by the other side instead of us, we'd release the entire exposé to the press immediately.

An hour later a messenger arrived with the official union statement. It delivered as much power as Paul had promised and then some. The pace things were moving at today took my breath away.

All of a sudden, I remembered my plans with Susan. *Shit.* I picked up the phone. The reception desk at GHQ answered, and I asked them to pass along a message to a Miss Susan Vogel:

"Tell her not to save me that seat after all." I also asked her to pass along my regrets that I wouldn't make it to the Augustines' watch party this eve. I was sad to be missing what was sure to be an enjoyable evening, but I knew I couldn't take my eye off the ball for even a second.

Next, I was onto my old pal from the *Chron* Jim Birch, letting him know he might have a scoop. He was raring to go and said he would reserve his first column of the week for the union's story.

By two, I was ready to type what I now called my "Notice of Pending Exposé on Establishing Power in El Salvador" By five, I'd also written my "Outline Points, Consolidation of Power in El Salvador." Then I decided I was ready to get back to a typewriter at Local 10. I took with me a couple of burgers, some fries, and a joe from a cafe across the street from the statue of St. Francis of Assisi that our union had helped bring to Frisco.

In due time, having been saved, as always, by an IBM electric typewriter you could do corrections on, I was ready to copy both items and to put them in mailers. I ran off three copies for Maria and friends, copies for Paul and each member of his uptown crew, copies for Father McGinnis and Tom, a copy for Frank, one for the safe, one for Jim Birch, one each for Susan and me, two for Dobbs, two for Reynolds, and two for the DOD.

These were the points I listed: The Hernandez Family Politics, IATG and Its Purchases, The Role of Tropic Steamship, and The Reagan Connection. Helped by the folders Doug had given me, I finished all of this by eight thirty. I had to postpone making copies of them to tomorrow, but I was able to get a copy to Frank's cubby.

Then it was over to the Archdiocese building to see Maria. The friends she was with only spoke Spanish. I struggled with a "Mucho buenas noches," unsure if that was the proper way to say it but trying to be polite.

Maria gave me the FUPS newsletter. I asked her how the *60 Minutes* piece was, saying I was sorry to have missed it. She frowned:

"It was terrible! No concern about the Reagan escalation of El Salvador, no exposure of the Carter administration's hypocrisy. It was all fluff."

Jim had been right after all. In my gut, I knew he would be. I offered an "adiós" all around and headed out into the sparkling night.

Sure enough, when I phoned around to Frank, Paul, and Susan, I found that Maria's opinion was unanimous: the piece was nothing but the government's line. I apologized to Susan for not following through on our plans.

"It's alright," she said, though her voice sounded a little hurt. "I hope you're giving 'em hell out there."

We agreed that we'd meet tomorrow for a tea and a joe at the International. By then it was near eleven, so I told her I was hitting the hay.

"Good luck," she said. "I don't know if I'll be able to sleep tonight. Tomorrow is… it's just so *big*. Defying the government… violating the union contract…risking *jail* time: It's all really happening."

I nodded to myself.

"It sure is."

47

Monday, December 22

I stood in the elevator of the ILWU building and pushed button 4, feeling a knot in my stomach large enough to tie down a cargo ship. Here it was. The media day.

The big conference room was engulfed by a swarm of bodies, some familiar, others not. I was pleased to see so many people I didn't know, because it meant they must have been out of town reporters.

Right away I spotted Susan talking to Maria Martinez, Sister Mary Margaret, and Sister Catherine Anne, so I went over to say my hellos. Susan explained that they had saved a seat for me, but they thought—rightly, I felt—that I should sit with the union crowd. I found a padded, straight-backed chair in the last row at the far side and took it, tipping my hat to some brothers and sisters from the union's clerk and warehouse locals.

Within a minute Frank arrived and made a beeline over to me, taking the seat next to mine.

"I took a look at the documents you prepared for the PCMA," he said to me. "Might be game-ending stuff."

"Maybe," I said, trying to remain cautious.

Then Paul came through the door, with union officers Bill Hanson, Joe Margolis, and Pete Turner in tow. They took the four chairs set out for them behind the podium. Also behind the podium were Father McGinnis, Tom Augustine, Rabbi Schwartz, Rev. Roger Morris and Minister John Boyer. The mass of reporters sat behind a conference table opposite the speakers, while the podium was flanked on either side by the media crews– newspaper and magazine folks recording audio, plus cameras from Channels 4, 5, and 7. Behind the media sat six rows of people from religious groups along with reps from our locals in northern Cal.

Once everyone was settled, Paul stood up and took his place at the podium, greeting everyone with a bright smile. He seemed darned smooth to me, a true leader. After introducing the other men behind the podium, he said that the West Coast dockworkers' union shared the view laid out in a letter by the now-deceased Archbishop of El Salvador, Oscar A. Romero, to President Carter. Paul noted that they'd find a copy of this letter in their press kit.

"To summarize, his and our view comes to this: because sending military aid to the junta of El Salvador will only lead to further oppression and violence, no more should be sent. It's that simple."

Paul then read our union's official statement, which was short, straightforward, and pretty darned bland, considering the junta's reign of terror. The statement made clear that we would not handle any military aid. It said that we did not take this action lightly, but it was decided after careful consideration of the union's policies and values. It ended by stating that we hoped our action would help end the nightmare of violence the people of El Salvador endured and aid them in their struggle for better lives, in which they possessed both freedom and security.

Paul went on to introduce Father McGinnis, adding that he was a close and much-valued friend who advocated relentlessly for peace and justice. Father McGinnis stood, smiled, and gave a wave, saying, "As you can see from our program—you'll find a copy of it in your kit— we religious peoples are here to commend most highly what the West Coast union of dockers has just announced." He went on to discuss the "dockworker union's deep and long-standing commitment to the struggle for social justice," contextualizing this announcement as just another example of that history.

Next on the podium was Tom Augustine. Tom presented some stirring and eloquent thoughts about the people of El Salvador. I was impressed and affected by the warmth in his words. Tom concluded:

"As another sign of our standing with the union of West Coast dockers, we will join hands tonight, at eight o'clock, with the members of its Local 10 and their families in their hiring hall, to bless them and their union. Everyone is cordially invited."

After the other speakers gave brief statements, Paul stood once more to thank everybody for coming and to invite them to stay for some coffee or tea.

"We hope to see you at eight" was his final remark.

Reporters gathered around Father McGinnis, Paul Murphy and Tom Augustine asking questions. Flash bulbs fired around the room as photographers scrambled for good shots of the committee members.

Susan came up to me and said she thought the event had been just perfect. I said I thought so, too, but before we got a chance to break it down, Betsy Palmer, the ILWU receptionist, approached and handed me a note. It read: *Dobbs from PCMA is asking for you. You can take it on 3, in Joe's office.*

Whenever we had a public event, we reserved that office and posted a sign on the door, saying UNION CALLS ONLY.

Susan and I each got on a phone, as I tried to guess what Dobbs might say. I couldn't tell from his voice if he was stressed.

"Morrow, I've just heard some–well, I've *heard*. To avoid any misunderstanding about the situation, we ought to meet as soon as we can. Two p.m. at my place is good for me."

I said that was no good, given that I had to help run the blessing scheduled for this evening. I suggested another way. If the minutes could read that we held a special meeting of the LRC (Labor Relations Committee) on Tuesday (tomorrow), he could do the hosting, so long as the union hosts the next three regular meetings.

It was no surprise when he balked at that. But I knew all his members' LRC reps would want to attend this meeting and would want to avoid meeting at Local 10. So it came as no surprise when his voice, though reluctant and grouchy, replied, "Okay."

After that call, Susan went back to the gathering to do some camera work, while I went into Paul's office, where a group of us had agreed to meet at one. First, we went around the room to discuss the media event, which everyone agreed had gone off without a hitch. Moving on, Paul announced that everyone supported the one-two punch plan he and I had discussed yesterday, including how I would proceed when meeting the PCMA tomorrow. That got a chorus of you bets and other affirmations.

Paul asked if there were any other points of business and, seeing no takers, he closed the meeting. I told Paul that I was still getting collected and that Susan and I would be at the local or on page. He said that, because we had a lot of guests, Susan and I shouldn't be gone too long, plus he wanted to meet at three or so to get to the latest tallies of support from faith-based groups. We nodded in agreement and I went to meet Susan back at my rig.

Susan and I listened to the radio on our way back to the local, and we heard some pretty good coverage of our announcement on KCBS.

48

Once Susan and I got to Local 10, I spent about an hour working on the speech I would deliver at the LRC meeting tomorrow: reading it, memorizing it, and rehearsing it, over and over. Susan took some snaps of the building and rapped with Shirley and Dolores for a while.

As I started to feel I knew the speech by heart, I got a beep from brother John Tilby at Pier 32. He sounded excited on the phone, saying that six tractors had just showed up to haul the trailers with the arms shipment over to the Oakland Army Terminal for dock storage there, and that "the whole thing looks like a replay of Chile in '78." I thanked John and told him I'd keep in touch. Then, with the knot back in my stomach, I passed the news on to Paul. All he said was, "Jesus."

But after that I got some good news. The current tally for wires of support came to 746! That meant that 746 religious leaders had expressed their unequivocal support for us. The breakdown on the West Coast was, for San Francisco, 63; for Los Angeles, 79; for Portland, 28; and for Seattle, 37. By eight, I'd have a typed list by region or state of all the folks who had wired their support, with their titles and names of their groups, to pass to Dobbs at the PCMA.

I couldn't wait to see the look on his face.

Unfortunately, after that was another blow. Shirley and Susan came in with a copy of today's *Chronicle*, fresh off the presses. We saw right away that our story was being downplayed. Jim Birch's name and byline were missing from the piece, which was very short. It had very clearly been squeezed onto page 3 at the last minute– far from the front-page headline we'd been hoping for. The article outlined that "the powerful West Coast union of dockers" had announced a "no" to military aid being sent to the junta of El Salvador. However, it failed to detail the horrors of the Salvadoran people. It wouldn't be enough to garner any major public support.

I got another beep, and soon Susan and I were on the phone. I asked the answering service guy if he knew who was on the line. He said with an exasperated laugh, "When I asked who's calling, the guy told me 'It's Mister Reynolds, and I'm in a hurry!' Whoever he is, he sure is a beaut."

Reynolds. The West Coast head of the Tropic Steamship Line. The meanest, most arrogant boss on the waterfront. A moment later his sour snarl was coming through on the other end of the phone.

"Is that you, Morrow?"

"Sure is."

"Well, I just saw you got *no* headline and *no* front page. Right?"

"Yeah, right."

"In fact, basically no press at all. And no support either. Reagan's about to take over, and all you got is a couple of churches who, everyone knows, are bleeding hearts."

"Just make sure you catch the meeting tomorrow, Reynolds."

"Jesus, Morrow, *I* won't be at that meeting. And, the fact is, I only called to warn you: you just don't have a hand to play."

"Well gee, Reynolds, thanks for your concern."

The phone clicked. I shook my head, smiled, and said, "I'll be damned."

Then I rang up Paul, who laughed as he said, "That's just what we want from Reynolds. I guess that piece is having some impact yet."

Towards the end of the workday, Frank, Susan, Shirley, Dolores and I decided to get some pizza and rap about the day's events. Things were moving so fast that I hadn't gotten a chance to discuss things in-depth with Frank recently, and I was eager to hear his thoughts. Frank thought it was really important that at the blessing tonight we stress the social context of the luxuries being delivered to the junta soldiers. He said Tom and Paul had come up with a "a real good plan" whereby each speaker would focus briefly on one of the many dimensions of the poverty of the larger population.

As Frank was finishing his description of the plan, someone knocked on his office window and hollered with a great laugh: "Hey, Frank! It's Elmer Young! Just in case you don't know, we're on page one in the *Oakland Tribune*."

When Frank heard that, he smiled broadly and hollered back, "You're a prince, and I'm getting the door!"

Elmer strode in with a real big smile and a paper in hand, its front page showing the reason for his excitement.

"Maybe I should've stopped here first," Elmer said, out-of-breath, "but I was late, and I only just now got dispatched for a job, but here it is, right on page one."

Frank was pretty smooth, smiling as he took the paper Elmer held out to him. Then he said, "So, join us for a bite and a beer and let me read it off?"

"Well," Elmer said. "I'm late in my seeing a lady, too, so maybe another time?"

Frank nodded his assent, saying, "In that case, I'll run a copy and you're on your way."

"I'm done with that part of the paper," Elmer said, "so you just keep it, and I'll keep the rest and hit the road. I just want to say, hey, right on to you all."

With a wide grin, he spun on his heels and headed out. Frank got back in gear and scanned the piece. The story noted the union's policy statement and quoted Paul Murphy on the junta's terror.

By now, it was close to six o'clock, when Father McGinnis, Tom, and the speakers were due to arrive. Frank smiled broadly as he opened the door for them, telling the ladies and myself to eat up. So that's what we did.

49

The hours leading up to my return to the union hall passed in a blur. After cleaning up, Susan and I walked to the main assembly hall to circulate. As we moved through the crowd, things seemed to whirl around me because of all the dockers, many of whom had family in tow. The folks who attended the monthly Social Justice Commission meetings at the Archdiocese came, bringing colleagues from all over town with them, many with buttons, leaflets, signs, and a local communist newspaper.

The sounds ricocheted off the bright acoustical dome under which we gathered. Somehow, amid all that hubbub, Susan spotted Doug Martin with his wife, Julie, and their boy. There were smiles all around when the boy, Matthew—who had been craning to see a nearby TV crew—shook my hand, smiled, and said, "Right on."

With Local 10's hall jammed with a lively and colorful crowd, Susan put her camera to work and took some snaps. Then we got to the chairs that Dolores, Shirley, and Frank had saved for us down front with the union crew. When we'd gotten squared away, with everyone exclaiming that this was "really some crowd," the blessing began.

Father McGinnis in his robes slowly walked down the center aisle beside Tom Augustine. They were followed by Rabbi Schwartz, dressed in black, walking beside John Gurley in his plain Dominican robe. A somber Sister Catherine Ann walked beside Sister Margaret, representing the slain Maryknoll nuns, and other representatives of the many faiths practiced in California followed behind them. TV cameras tracked them and camera flashes lit up the room as the entourage made their way to the stage. It was very dramatic.

The representatives of faith stood side by side on the stage facing the audience, their arms locked together as at a protest. A long line of moral courage. Somber. Defiant. Determined. It was a profound and moving assembly of the devout.

Tom did a fine job introducing the reason for their presence. Paul's short, passionate speech about the ILWU's statement of conscience made me proud of our union. The lighting, music and color amplified the emotion of the speakers, making their words resonate all the more deeply with the crowd. It was just like the gathering at Mission Dolores church a few weeks ago: a mix of laughter, sorrow, hope, faith, dread and despair joined in one powerful and collective voice. We all felt truly connected to everyone else in that hall and to the many people who couldn't be there.

Father McGinnis stepped forward, raised one hand and blessed all who stood up for peace and justice. Who stood against cruelty and hate and oppression. He reminded us all, "blessed are the peacemakers." And he thanked us for our commitment to the people of El Salvador.

As he finished the blessing, the entire room joined him in one solemn, holy word of affirmation: "*AMEN!*"

After that the scene seemed to swirl and blur even more. I shimmied through the crowd over towards Frank, wanting to tell him what a great job he'd done. When I finally got his ear, he smiled and thanked me, then said:

"Tomorrow is your big day, Steve. I think it's best that you go home and get some sleep."

When he said that, it suddenly hit me just how tired I was. My body seemed to sag towards the ground. I mean I was totally knackered. I told Frank some sleep sounded good, adding a "See you mañana."

But in the end, I stayed to praise the good work so many of the folks had done. Paul, Pete, Bill, Joe, Tom, and Father McGinnis, Maria Martinez, Sister Catherine and Sister Margaret…Men and women I was honored to call friends.

Susan and I confirmed our plans for the morning. She would be at the local no later than eight for any fine-tuning and to help me with my response to the pitiful coverage in the *Chron*. We'd be at the PCMA by nine thirty, the meeting there would last two hours or so, and then we would head back to the local.

She looked me in the eye and placed her hand on my shoulder.

"Now, I think, you should go home," she said.

I nodded. It must have been obvious to everyone I was exhausted. Or maybe just the people who cared about me.

I got home to my couch and poured a drink just as the news at ten began. Our media event that morning kicked off the show. It showed Paul reading from our statement refusing to handle weapons. Then there were some fast shots of the blessing, which the reporter called an "interfaith service."

The reporter said that numerous local religious leaders had expressed strong support for the union. The camera panned for shots around the hall, and the reporter ended by saying that, though our contract prohibited any such boycott action, the employer group had thus far said, "No comment." That last statement was no surprise.

On that note, I decided to hit the hay. As I lay in bed, I flashed back briefly on scenes from what I then realized had been a really super day. A whole lot of work by a whole lot of folks was surely starting to come together.

My last thought before drifting off to sleep was of the volunteers, unknown to me, who would be up all night typing the updated list of religious supporters for me to receive at eight the next morning for the big meeting with the PCMA and the Tropic Steamship company goons.

Presente

Would the press coverage of the blessing and the dirt we'd dug up about the arms shipment be enough to turn them around? I had to wait for the morning sun to burn through the San Fran fog to find out.

50

Tuesday, December 23

When the alarm sounded at 6:15, I bounded out of bed. My sleep had been shallow and fitful, interrupted by thoughts of the day ahead, so I was eager to finally get to it. I dressed as fast as I could, went out, and grabbed the *Chron*.

Nothing on page one.

I turned the page. Then again. Then again. Eventually, I found a short piece buried at the bottom of page 10. My annoyance deepened when, scanning the article, I came across a complete lie. An unnamed government source said that "The first cargo affected was a relatively small shipment of batteries and vehicle parts waiting at Pier 30." It really riled me up to see these blatant lies intended to manipulate the public against our cause printed in the press. At the same time, I knew this could play right into my hands at the LRC meeting today.

Reading further, I saw that the piece didn't even mention last night's blessing, noting only that the union had been "lauded by several prominent clergymen." Also of note (if unsurprising): the article said the PCMA had announced that our refusal breaks our contract's no-strike pledge, so members who refused to work the cargo to El Salvador would not receive pay.

The piece did end with a strong comment from Paul Murphy: "This boycott will continue until the rulers of El Salvador can clearly demonstrate some compassion towards their own people. If just one person's life is saved by all this, then it will be worth it." But the weak coverage did not bode well for my upcoming meeting with the PCMA.

Back at my place, I was pouring myself a joe when a call came through from Dobbs, the local PCMA head, who confirmed that the shipment had been drayed over to the Oakland Army Terminal, as we thought. He also said that, because it hadn't been booked for shipping, only its trailer numbers were available.

"So, no booking or itemizing at all," he continued. "That's where we'll have to start. But we also confirmed with the OAT staff that the shipment is what the *Chronicle* says it is– a small consignment of vehicle parts and batteries."

I suggested, partly to see if he really believed what he'd gotten from his source, that we start off with an exchange of paper. I show him mine, he shows me his. He said that was fine by him. He then said that Herman Reynolds, head of Tropic Steamship Company, would send a lieutenant to the meeting today, but that no rep from the DOD would be there.

"They must be really confident," I scoffed.

"They must be," he replied.

I told Dobbs I'd see him at ten, and that I'd be "bringing along a brand-new hire who's doing research for the uptown crew at Franklin." With the cover set for Susan, I hung up.

Soon after, I was walking into Local 10. Dolores gave me the rundown: Frank Spaulding and Jimmy Fletcher were with the dispatchers, while Ron Curtice and Gordon Wright were down at Pier 15 to listen to the testing of the first of Joe Montieth's new lifts, but they'd all be back for our noon debrief.

I walked into my office to find Susan already waiting for me.

"Game day, boss" she said playfully. "What can I do to help?"

I smiled at her enthusiasm, handed her the paperwork I had prepared for today's meeting, and asked her to make copies: two for Dobbs, two for Reynolds, and two for the DOD.

"Then, if you could put other copies into mailers– three for Maria Martinez, one for Frank, one for the safe, one for Paul, and one each for Father McGinnis and Tom."

"So, fourteen overall?" she immediately replied.

"Quick math."

As Susan went off, I did some last-minute practice of my rap for today. I thought I was prepared for anything they could throw on me, but there was a lot riding on this meeting today, and I knew my fellow workers were relying on me.

Fast as lightning, Susan was back with the files and we were on the road.

Game day indeed.

51

Pulling up to the PCMA gate, a cheery attendant told me that my rig would be parked.

"This is real service," I said to Susan.

We took the elevator to the second floor, where we found a crowd of maybe seventy-five people. The conference room was vast, with posh furnishings. On one side was a line of upholstered swivel chairs for Dobbs, his PCMA staff and representatives of Tropic Steam. The other side of the table had this same seating arrangement. We normally used the space for what we call a "fishbowl negotiation" of our coastwide longshore contract, with the union on one side and the PCMA on the other.

This time, however, it was just me and Susan on one otherwise empty side of the table, facing opposite Dobbs and his swarm. I wondered if someone had been hired to design the most intimidating room possible. The high walls, dark colors, and swirling seating arrangement made someone sitting in the middle of it all feel incredibly small. Good for intimidation tactics, I should think.

Seated next to Dobbs was one of Reynolds's stooges, Roger P. Rogers, who I thought was not the worst of the Tropic Steamship bunch. I introduced Susan as we took our seats, and Dobbs shot back with a snarl: "Just so you know, neither Reynolds nor anyone from the DOD has shown up."

I waved that off and said, "Well in that case, why don't we just get started?"

I slid to him a copy of our refusal. Somebody snapped a photo of me as I did so. *Documenting the messenger carrying the bad news,* I thought. Dobbs slid a document back to me, which basically repeated what he'd told me on the phone this morning. He then handed me an envelope.

"This came for you as we got to our chairs," he said.

It was a mailer from Tom Augustine. Before I could open it, Dobbs proceeded:

"As you can plainly see in our statement, the OAT has confirmed by phone that the shipment is batteries and vehicle parts. Not guns. Not tanks. *Batteries.* Put simply, the shipment will stand. It will stand because of its contents and its small size, neither of which is headline news. Plus, Reagan will soon be inaugurated as president. So, given that you don't have a leg to stand on, can you advise us on what to expect now? I feel like you've already wasted enough of everybody's time."

Taking that invitation, I nodded slowly.

"First, I'll distribute a few copies of our outline about what is *actually* contained in the aid shipment. I'll ask you to read that copy aloud so that everyone in the PCMA can hear and it be added to our official minutes. I want to add that all our info is substantiated with evidence going back to December Third, the day one of our members found the aid. I've been keeping detailed records, in date-specific folders ever since."

Dobbs took my materials and asked one of his staffers to make a hundred copies for the rest of the PCMA observers. Then he began to read the report aloud, starting with my introductory notes and eventually landing on the full list of everything in the aid shipment.

"Folder Number 1, Safety and Rescue Equipment parts and accessories, for the following weapons: M-1, M-2 carbine, Colt .45 twelve gauge pump, M-14, M-15, M-60 light machine gun; Folder Number 2, Radio Equipment; Folder Number 3…"

This went on for about 5 unbroken minutes. The tension in the room built, eyes turned to me, and Dobbs' voice became more and more bitter as he listed off grenades, body armor, and practically every weapon under the sun, painting a starkly different picture to what he had claimed just moments ago.

When he had finished, the room fell silent. None of them wanted to claim for certain that my list was untrue. I think they could tell by the look in my eyes that I could prove it. As I started opening my mailer from Tom Augustine I began my key statement:

"Given the moral questions involved, we received massive support for our refusal, especially from the religious community. Individuals and groups in the United States and elsewhere. The union and social justice commission maintain the tallies up to date, and I have just been sent a mailer of the latest figures. Dobbs, would you care to read them for the group?"

Dobbs took the page with a sour look on his face, shaking his head as if he were rejecting what he read.

"U.S. Support, December 23, 3:00 a.m. Individual Religious, 1,332; Religious Groups, 765; West Coast Support, Individual Religious, Seattle, 65; Portland, 45; San Francisco, 73; Los Angeles, 107; Religious Groups, Seattle, 43; Portland, 23; San Francisco, 49; Los Angeles, 62."

Gasps rang throughout the room. Even I was surprised it had gotten that high since last I checked. Tom's mailer ended with a note that similar tallies were being kept for other countries all around the world.

After a few moments of flummoxed silence, Dobbs asked if he could have a few minutes to "get all these papers copied and distributed among the observers." I said of course, and Susan and I got up and excused ourselves.

Round 1 had gone to us.

52

One joe and a trip to the can later, Susan and I were called back to hear from Dobbs. I immediately saw that he and his side had become more serious.

"I thought that we would caucus pretty quick, based on what we have now," Dobbs stated, "but first we want to hear what we can expect from the union."

I resumed where I had left off, noting as I spoke that their side was becoming even more sober.

"Firstly, I know we would refuse to load the cargo and put the bosses through a couple rounds of arbitration. And with the press and TV folks surely being out in force by then, we could well choose to go to court for another round. Maybe even a couple rounds. We will make it clear that our longshore folks refuse to handle the aid on moral grounds and personal conscience. In other words, individual dockers have their own morals. They don't want to work cargo that is destined to be used by a military junta to kill its own people.

"For that reason, if the union is forced to arbitrate or go to court, the PCMA and Tropic Steam would be seen as trying to muscle dockworkers to undertake work they view as immoral. Those workers could invoke the Nuremberg Court's judgment, from 1946. Those judges rejected the Nazi military leaders' claims that they were simply 'following orders.' They declared those soldiers had the duty to refuse to obey immoral orders. And with huge numbers of religious people and groups citing that, too, things could get explosive.

"In short: if it comes to an on-the-job refusal, that won't be any fun for you. Our sources have guaranteed that."

Dobbs asked what our sources said.

"First, the groups involved in Seattle, Portland, and Los Angeles will hold demonstrations in and around the PCMA's and Tropic Steam's offices. Locally, demonstrations will include speeches, pickets, and vigils on your front steps. There's also talk of sit-ins, complete with priests and nuns, monks and preachers, rabbis, and Buddhist monks. Not a great image for your gang. I've also heard that some folks are being trained to lock arms and arrange themselves in tight groups that only a tactical squad might be able to break up so that the squad can drag individual protesters off to a police wagon.

"Picture this on television: a nun, seventy-five years old or so, who has locked arms with a rabbi, and a black man of the cloth, all three being dragged and pushed out of place and hauled off to jail. If that scene appears on the telly and in the press, I would expect a strong public reaction.

"Now, I don't want to step on any toes here. But as far as I'm aware, the PCMA is a conglomeration of one hundred and twenty member groups, correct? And of those hundred and twenty, only one member is involved in this situation. And that one member is actually an East Coast marginal member that nobody likes. So, I can't help but wonder: do you *really* want to plant your flag and defend Tropic Steam's hill?"

Dobbs took a moment to consider this and came back to me with a laughable understatement. "In other words, you expect this situation to spread and escalate?"

"Ha, wouldn't you? Plus, folks of the cloth protesting are one thing, but protests against arming Salvadoran strongmen who, let's not forget, just murdered four American *nuns*, could just explode! I mean, what do you think is gonna happen when the students are back in Berkeley? Those kids are already fed up with Reagan and his crowd. You could face a real wildfire, there. Those kids don't go in for all this 'write to your Congressman' malarkey, they take to the streets."

I stopped and looked around, giving everyone a questioning look. After a pause, Dobbs said his side wanted to caucus. I knew that Rogers wasn't there only to take notes for Tropic Steamship. I was pretty sure he'd have to explain his company's actions to the rest of the PCMA reps assembled, and they had looked mighty pissed off when they heard the list of weapons in the "aid" package.

During this break, I took a couple snaps of Susan while she gave her thoughts on the meeting.

Posing for the camera, she said, "I shouldn't have been surprised that a bunch of executives from shipping corporations don't care much what longshoremen think. Or even about the cargo, for that matter. Clearly, they're in it for exactly one reason– the money. So, who cares what's being shipped?"

After about ten minutes of chatting, I told Susan that I wanted to cut short their caucus.

"How will you do that?" she asked.

I took a sheet of paper and an envelope from the stock kept in the lounge and wrote a note to Dobbs. The note said that because we wanted to keep our discussion under wraps for now, I'd held back on the more explosive stuff. Now, I'd like to meet in private this time with him, Reynolds, *and* the DOD. I handed the note to Dobbs' secretary, and within a couple of minutes, we were called back into the conference room.

Dobbs looked like his wife had just left him, his dog had died and he was scheduled for extensive dental work. He looked me up and down and, through gritted teeth, said: "We need some more time before we come to a decision. How about we take a break and reconvene in an hour?"

I beamed up at him. "Okay on all scores."

Dobbs stood up and walked away without another word.

Round 2 to me.

***

Forty-five minutes later, Dobbs ushered Susan and me into a small room and said he'd be right back with Rogers, the Tropic Steamship rep. Dobbs returned a moment later and started talking even quicker:

"Okay, we've gotten a hold of the bills of lading, and, while there are still a few things I need to take a closer look at, I am now starting to suspect that I, the *Chronicle* and possibly even Reynolds, may have all been duped by the DOD and the OAT."

I replied that Reynolds and Tropic Steam, with the help of the consignee of the aid shipment and a trade group here in San Francisco, were engaged in some shocking stuff on behalf of the junta and the Reagan folks.

I then asked if I could meet with him and Reynolds and a DOD rep off the record and unannounced, in his office at five. He balked, so I shook my head, saying:

"If that's out, then we will advise you and your side that the union will release all of our information, including the Steamship complicity in representing the weapons as non-lethal aid. You tell Reynolds that if he wants to keep his job and even save Tropic Steam from itself, he should hear what I've got to say and see our proof, which he can do when we meet at five."

Another sigh of defeat from Dobbs: "Yeah, okay. I'll hear you then with whoever."

Susan and I made our way back to the lot, where the parking attendant brought my rig to us. We gave him a generous tip and thanked him for my newly clean windshield, then bolted.

After we had told Shirley and Dolores that things had gone well, the four of us got to Frank's office to give him, Jim Birch, Ron Curtice, Gordon Wright, and Jimmy Fletcher the same report. I figured to save time by reporting right away, by speaker phone, to Paul and his crew, Father McGinnis, and Tom at the same time. They all congratulated me on a job well done, which felt good to hear.

Then Paul shared some great news. He said that the *Oregon Journal*, which had just hit the streets in Portland, had basically reprinted the piece from the *Chron*, including this near quote: "The first cargo affected was a small shipment of batteries and vehicle parts waiting at the San Francisco waterfront." Now every one of those lies printed just played right into my hand with Dobbs, Tropic Steam and the DOD.

We broke the meeting with high spirits. Those of us in the office took a quick moment to recuperate and enjoy some extra-large pizzas and soda.

53

Once we'd recuperated and were ready for our next round with the other side, Susan and I hopped in the rig and speeded over to Dobbs' office. A staffer ushered us in to Dobbs' first-floor corner office which he, with a smarmy laugh, always called his "office suite." It had upscale furnishings and a wet bar that he insisted with yet another laugh was "strictly for business purposes."

Dobbs was seated in the executive chair at his large, tidy desk. Tropic Steamship's Vice President Reynolds and his henchman, Rogers, who clearly had been there for a while, were sitting on straight-backed chairs at a table off to Dobbs' right. On the other side loomed another figure who I presumed was from the DOD. This assumption was proven correct when Dobbs introduced the man, a Mr. Boroughs.

Once we'd gotten settled, I was about to speak when Dobbs waved his hand at me.

"Excuse me, Morrow, but I've already run a copy of your 'Notice' for Mister Boroughs, and Rogers has done the same for Reynolds. We're all up to speed. So you can skip your usual routine and get straight to the point."

I just smirked and nodded.

"Alright then. I wanted to meet with only you three folks so that I could fully explain why you should want the government to cancel the aid in question. To avoid wasting time, I'll give each of you a couple copies of my outline points and give Dobbs this case of folders, which includes the sequence of evidence corresponding to each of our points. We'll save time if your side makes copies of this evidence for both Tropic Steam and the DOD as you read our points aloud."

I got up to hand Dobbs copies of our points. He sighed, hesitating, before he began to read the outline typed on the page, under the heading "the Consolidation of Power in El Salvador."

Even just the subject list illustrated so much of my journey over the past few weeks, and so much of the political context that had been building towards this moment. It read:

1. Building the Junta by Means of Oppression and Suppression
2. Payment Rendered to the Officer Class for Services
3. Payment to the Death Squads for Services
4. Origins and Nature of the U.S. Connection
    a. Family of General M. Hernandez
    b. Hernandez Brigade
    c. The Hernandez Family's Division of Labor
    d. Mr. G. Hernandez Comes to San Francisco
    e. The Role of the Junta Consulate
    f. The Role of the Immigration and Naturalization Service
    g. The Founding of FUPS (United Salvadoran Patriotic Forces) and the Role of El Salvador's Consulate in San Francisco
    h. The Politics and Funding of FUPS (United Salvadoran Patriotic Forces)
    i. The Founding of the Inter-American Trade Group (IATG) by its owner, Mr. G. Hernandez
    j. IATG, the Purchasing Agent of Luxury Goods and Items for the Junta's Officer Class and Death Squads
    k. IATG Bills of Lading
    l. The Role of Tropic Steam and Vice President Herman Reynolds in the Business Transactions of IATG
    m. Storage and Distribution of IATG Goods by 'Mr. T.

Hernandez,' brother of G. Hernandez and consignee of the weapons in question here under his military name, "Col. T. Hernandez"

n. The Reagan Cold War and the Business Growth of IATG and Tropic Steam

o. The Role of G. Hernandez in the Christian Radical Right

p. The Roles of G. Hernandez and Herman Reynolds in the Reagan Campaign

q. The Roles of G. Hernandez and Herman Reynolds in a state GOP Inaugural Celebration.

I could see that all four men sitting opposite me were quite shaken. Dobbs then read one more sentence: "A Note to the Reader: G. Hernandez buys a great many things from firms throughout the United States, all of which are shipped from San Francisco's Mission Rock Terminal (Pier 50) or from docks in Seattle or Los Angeles. A list of those firms is available."

I proceeded to lay out my case:

"Because Reynolds and Boroughs unfortunately could not be with us this morning, allow me to clarify that none of what you just saw has been shown to the rest of the PCMA, the press, or the public at large. You are the first four people outside the union to see it."

"I feel honored," Dobbs huffed wryly to himself.

"If the shipment is allowed to proceed," I said, "this second part of our exposé will go to the press along with what you got this morning. Were that to happen, our supporters are talking about a total and complete boycott of Tropic Steam's booking offices—for freight, resorts, cruises, and travel agencies. In other words, if we made all the evidence public, all of Tropic's many assets would become multiple targets."

With that, I turned with a pointed pause towards Reynolds.

The man was blanching. His face seemed to further whiten the longer I waited. I continued, driving my point home.

"Our bottom line–I'll say it slow so that you can write it down: Get the shipment canceled and on the road to the Sharpe Depot, for shipment east, by 3:00 p.m. tomorrow, or this exposé about weapons of war and luxury goods will be front page for a week or so, starting on Christmas Day, when the *Examiner* will publish it in a special noontime edition."

As the words came out of my mouth, they really did feel like a bomb. Our team had deliberated on the deadline. We decided that, because of the strong support we already had and what we can prove with certainty, the best time to publish our exposé is the moment when we announce our boycott of Tropic Steam. We know that many church services on Christmas morning would almost certainly include a mention of it. With this new wrinkle, we decided that the timing of our ultimatum—three o'clock on Christmas Eve—was more than fair.

As I finished my ultimatum, Dobbs got a buzz. I told him to go ahead, so he picked up the phone and called. After listening for a few moments, he placed the phone down on the desk and looked at me.

"Looks like your uptown team has something to say."

My heart raced. Dobbs put the phone on speaker and soon Paul's voice was ringing through. He had another bombshell–but this time, it was directed at me.

Paul said: "The *Examiner* just put out a piece on our action where they interviewed the head guy in FUPS. He's quoted as claiming our refusal is 'irresponsible and against the interests of democracy'."

My jaw dropped. From our research on FUPS, I knew what this was–a signal used to mark targets for death squads and other violent attacks. The junta's goons in the States were threatening to come after the ILWU. Including me.

"Frank's drafting a statement to advise our ranks on what that statement means," Paul continued, "But I thought you should know right away."

I thanked Paul and told him we'd speak later. Dobbs hung up the phone while he and his associates exchanged puzzled looks. Paul had been sure to use some code of his own to talk about this new threat so as not to weaken my position with the bigwigs.

"Now who in the goddamn hell are these FUPS?" Reynolds grouched.

"The United Salvadoran Patriotic Forces. I suggest you read the section on them in my exposé. But let's not get distracted. I believe I made some demands."

"Some threats, more like."

"Look," I ploughed on, "if the aid is canceled, as I just set out, we won't rub it in by making an announcement at another media event. And if some reporter follows up, we'll say only that we know the shipment was canceled and taken off the dock. We'd have to report it briefly to the membership in our union paper, but that would only touch on what's in the public record as of this morning.

"Finally–and let me slow down here so you can get it down as a quote–if we learn that *any* such aid is again being booked in one of our ports, or that junta agents are trying to track our sources, or that Reagan has ordered a troop intervention, we'll pass *everything* we've got to the media. With updates."

Boroughs, the Department of Defense rep and an altogether shady figure who looked like an ex-Marine that had gone soft, leaned over to Dobbs and whispered something inaudible in his ear. Dobbs nodded, then faced me.

"However this gets settled," he said, "it cannot include any talk about lying by the DOD. I mean, you can't tell the public that."

"Why not? The DOD sure as heck did lie!"

"But that would really look bad."

"Why is that *my* problem?" I exclaimed. But then, being more tactical, I gave them this:

"Look, if somebody comes to ask whether you lied, there's nothing to stop you from just lying again. Tell them you didn't lie, somebody… misunderstood the information. Tell them this shipment was really meant for Korea, or Taiwan, or Antarctica for all I care."

I was shocked when he just frowned, shook his head, and said: "Maybe we could do something like that…" But I kept my poker face.

With that exchange and given our deadline, I thought Dobbs was ready to move along.

He asked, "So, this is it, or what?"

I said, "Yeah. For now."

"Okay, then we'll caucus with the rest of the group. But first, the three of us here also need to caucus for ten minutes."

Susan and I tried to walk out calmly, despite what was going on in our heads. She got another tea with lemon and, I, a cup of joe. Then I called Paul and Frank to give a brief, exciting report. I asked Paul if he could arrange the tallies from around the world, as well as some of the best wires from the US, to be sent care of Dobbs in an hour or so. He readily agreed.

"Let's bring this thing home, brother," he said.

Then we turned to the issue of how to stand down.

"If they concede now, they probably won't put their answer in writing," Paul said. "But given all the proof we've accumulated, we could live with that and accept a verbal agreement."

I agreed. I thanked him again for the warning about the FUPS and said we'd talk soon.

I sat back next to Susan, who looked truly exhilarated by this whole experience. I raised my cup and smiled to her.

"Looks like you might be home in time for Christmas after all."

She looked down at her feet and replied, "Yes, I guess I might."

I found myself searching for some sign of hesitation in her voice. In spite of all the promises I'd made to myself about Susan, I couldn't help but want her to stay. But she was totally inscrutable.

"Hey," I said, "how would you feel about a supper at Tadich's Grill? Best seafood in town, and it's practically an historical landmark in Frisco."

"I'm game!" she swiftly responded.

After a few more minutes of waiting, Dobbs' secretary approached us. "The others are ready."

I looked at Susan, who gave me an encouraging wink and a smile that tamped down my anxiety a bit. We went back into the conference room, my whole body tingling with anticipation. This was it. The moment of truth. Dobbs, Reynolds, Rogers and Boroughs each had his eyes fixed ahead in an angry glare, but I dared not allow myself to read anything into their expressions. Susan and I took our seats. She gave me an encouraging squeeze on the leg, then folded her hands on the table. We waited in silent anticipation.

"Well, Morrow," Dobbs grumbled, "it looks like you've won."

54

Right after Dobbs admitted defeat, he said they still had to caucus with the rest of the DOD, Tropic Steam and the PCMA. He asked that I come back at 8 that evening. Still, these were the main players. To have them give in was, put simply, a giant victory.

I left the room to call Paul and give him the news. He was thrilled and promised to spread the word. Susan and I retrieved our jackets and walked arm in arm past Sansome and Battery, a little giddy. No words could express my happiness-or my relief-and I think Susan felt the same.

Down a short block, we came to a building with a brass plaque that identified our destination: the Tadich Grill. The plaque said that the Tadich Grill had been designated a state and city historical business site and had first opened on the waterfront in 1849. It had moved a couple times because of landfill along the shore of the bay, the 1906 earthquake, and more recently, urban redevelopment. The last move had brought the restaurant back to a site close to where it had first been situated.

It felt like an apt place for a celebration meal.

We walked through swinging wooden doors attached with brass fittings. Not wanting to wait in line, I smiled to the maître d' and asked for "Two at the bar," by raising two fingers. He gave us a broad smile, and with a wave, invited us to sit "halfway down."

Soon after, Susan raised the Manhattan she had ordered, and, with a smile, toasted: "Cheers to us!"

I raised my own glass, a vodka on the rocks, and whispered: "To the union!"

Once we'd ordered, we returned to the subject of Susan's trip home.

"Even if the PCMA changes its tune and tries to go ahead with the aid shipment or Tropic Steam ignores our deadline, you might still depart on one of the flights you've booked, since Paul and his crew might take our fallback position and postpone an escalation. That also would mean that, once you returned to San Francisco, you'd be ready for the *Moon* or whatever else happens."

Before she had a chance to respond, my beeper went off. It was from Dobbs. I took another sip of my drink, then hit the payphone (with my last dime!) and called him back.

"If you're at supper you can finish up, but make sure to be here no later than seven-thirty," he told me. I didn't take kindly to being spoken to so rudely, but I was so eager to get this whole thing settled I let it slide.

"Alright. The earlier the better."

Then he mentioned what I took to be his actual reason for calling. Dobbs said that he, his guests, and their DOD contacts in Washington wanted to have our latest tallies right away. He asked if I could call to arrange for that. I told him I'd already made that call and he could expect the tallies by the time we were back.

Then I heard two words that didn't often come out of Dobbs' mouth:

"Thank you."

I reported all this to Susan over the two glasses of house white wine we ordered to complement our meals. While we were puzzled at the other side's impatience and wanted to close the deal, we still managed to enjoy our food. As we ate, we recalled some of the times we'd shared and the rush of the whole exciting affair. It was a wonderful supper.

We continued to reminisce on the walk back to the PCMA, but the seriousness of what we were walking back to started to weigh us down as we drew nearer our destination. Our hearty chuckles became weary laughs.

First, we met briefly with Dobbs, Reynolds, and Boroughs out in the lobby. They then guided us back into the conference room. There, seventeen people already were seated on his side of the table. I had met most of them briefly at one time or another but knew none of them well.

Dobbs began by handing me a mailer.

"This came for you, as you promised."

I opened Paul's mailer. I passed two of its three documents to Dobbs, sliding the third to Susan.

"Do you explain or do I?" I asked. Susan turned to Dobbs and replied: "I think he can explain well enough."

I thought she was just dynamite.

Dobbs took a sip of his water, cleared his throat, and slowly, nervously, started reading off the figures. "US Religious Community, Groups. 1,784; Officers, 3,714; Laity, 26,348."

For the next ten straight minutes, Dobbs was forced to sit there and rattle off similarly astonishing figures from all over the globe. Not only that, he read off wires from prominent figures and groups voicing their vehement support for us. Maryknoll Sisters, Ursuline Sisters, the Congressional Black Caucus, the Machinists Union, Woodworkers of America, Amnesty International. The list just went on and on.

After about ten minutes, Dobbs demurred.

"Alright, alright, I think this is enough. We'll make copies for everyone present to see the rest."

"Just one second," I interjected. "I want to point something out. Could you take a look under the subheading 'Monterey, California' in the list of religious groups you've got there?"

When he had found the tally, he looked up, puzzled.

"What am I looking for here?"

"Down the list a bit, you'll see that we got a wire from a convent of Carmelite nuns."

"So? What about it?"

"So, they sent us a wire–but they don't even *talk!*"

I thought my comment was better than anyone else seemed to think it. But when I heard Susan clearing her throat, I figured maybe they weren't the most pious bunch of guys.

Dobbs was done talking. He was licked and he knew it. He ended the meeting exactly as Paul had predicted.

"We're putting nothing in writing, but we'll give you a call."

There was nothing left for me to say.

55

I drove Susan back to her rental car in our lot at North Point, my mind whirling the whole way. I pulled into the space right next to her car, and we got to our final plan. If there was news of an official answer, I'd ring her, no matter the time. But if no call came before seven tomorrow morn, I'd ring her then.

"And what about goodbyes?" she asked.

"Goodbyes?"

She said that whether her flight would be on United at three fifteen, on Delta at ten forty-five or on Continental at five to five, she'd have to make the rounds at Local 10, the international crew at Franklin Street, and the archdiocesan building.

"There's just so many people I need to see. The Painters, to thank them for hosting me this whole time. And Frank, Shirley and Dolores. Jimmy Fletcher, Charlie Wilson, Gordon Wright, and Ron Curtice. Paul, Tom and Father McGinnis."

I said I could arrange all that. The painful reality of her departure was starting to sink in. I think I even saw a tear in her eye. It all just seemed so hurried and chaotic. So…unreal.

"No matter what, I need to be in the airport for my check-in no later than one-thirty. There you and I can have a much-too-hurried drink. And then I want to be at my gate by two-thirty, for our own private goodbye."

My whole drive home that night, I wondered what the heck "our private goodbye" meant. I guess only time could tell.

Back at my place, I made all the arrangements for Susan's goodbye, and gave a full rundown of the day's events to trusty old brother-in-arms, Frank Spaulding. We were in high spirits, anticipating that in spite of all the odds three weeks ago, all our hard work was going to pay off.

Then I rang my reporter on the inside, Jim Birch, to report on my meetings. He had news of his own:

"I've finally got through to them at the *Chron*, Steve! Everything I've written so far they've completely butchered, but I've just finished a blistering piece on the aid, and I've convinced them to run it!"

He also had begun a piece for "a Sunday noon special edition," which he said the *Chron*'s editor and the City Desk were really pleased about, calling it "a six-day page one shocker."

I encouraged him, saying, "Right on!" It excited me that someone was finally going to get our story out there. Jim thanked me for giving him such a great story, and I thanked him for all the work he's done trying to get it out there, which I knew was not easy. We agreed that, come tomorrow, we'd be in touch.

By then, it was time for me to hit the hay. Despite the heady day and the million things still on my mind, I fell asleep as soon as my head hit the pillow.

56

Talk about being startled from sleep! As I reached up to answer the ringing phone, I saw the time on the clock was 4:35 A.M. The caller was Dobbs. First thing he said was that I should take notes and he'd go slow.

"Good morning to you, too," I mumbled as I reached for a pen. When I told Dobbs I was ready, he began on what was clearly a carefully prepared speech.

"The Pacific Coast Marine Association has fully discussed the situation, by speaker phone, with sitting members of the Reagan Administration's transition team at the Department of Defense. These discussions finished at 3:05 a.m. The U.S. government's cancelation of the aid shipment is a virtual certainty. The DOD and PCMA agreed to a common statement for possible use at 2:45 a.m. Therefore, the PCMA requests the ILWU immediately cease further action in regard to said shipment. The chair–that's me, Dobbs–to call back when San Francisco recommendations have been approved or amended by the union.

"Although the PCMA put nothing on paper, Tropic Steamship will cancel the shipment at 6:00 a.m., San Francisco time. At 7:00 a.m., this proposal having been accepted in its entirety, OAT will start to contract independent truckers to haul the trailers to the Sharpe Depot, with hook-ups and preparation starting at 8:00 a.m. and hauling time at 9:00 a.m. Once the shipment is dismantled, the components will be sent by rail to four East Coast supply depots to be inventoried."

What a wake-up call.

Once Dobbs finished, I read back to him what I'd jotted down. He said it was all okay and then reported that the head of the PCMA was reading to Paul what Dobbs had just read to me. He said they hoped to get the union's acceptance sometime before seven this morning. I acknowledged, "Yeah, okay," before he added that I should get ready again.

As "a courtesy," the PCMA thought we'd like to know what they were planning to say when asked about its unannounced cancellation of the shipment. So Dobbs read me the party line.

"Recently and for the first time, the DOD planned to ship, via a West Coast port, in a commercial vessel flying the U.S. flag, some military aid authorized for El Salvador during the previous fiscal year. When the economies of sending that military aid, as part of a different aid package and on a different routing, were calculated, that shipment was canceled."

I thought that sounded like a load of hooey, and the public would surely see right through it. But all I said was: "That's fine, Dobbs. Keep in touch."

I made myself an instant joe, then readied to call Paul. Of course, just as I reached for the phone, he called me.

"Congratulations, Steve."

The whole thing started to feel real. We'd won! The enormous weight that had been crushing me these past few weeks started to lift, and even though it was the early morning, I suddenly felt more awake than I had in a long time. I always lived for the thrill of beating the bosses in a dispute, but this felt like so much more. If felt like we had done something that could have an impact on the course of history, and for the better.

Paul and I agreed the DOD's plan to handle things was shabby, especially that whole "economies" line.

"Just plastering one lie over another," I said.

We decided that we should get a conference call going. He called Joe Margolis, Pete Turner and Bill Hanson, while I called Frank Spaulding, Tom Augustine, and Susan (who practically screamed in excitement when I gave her the news).

When our pre-dawn conference call began, Paul raised an interesting point, saying it was surprising that they gave us a deadline of seven for our response. Their demand for such a quick turnaround might indicate that they weren't sure we'd buy their proposal, and wanted time to make another should we refuse.

Considering that, Paul thought we might try to string them out to maybe eight or so. It would make it clear that we were the ones in the driver's seat and give the impression that it was a hard sell to our partners to call off our "powerful exposé" (those were his words, and they made me proud). He summarized his tactic:

"We want them to remember how hard this was for them, how close to disaster they came, so they think twice about trying something like this in the future."

We all agreed. After that I wanted to call Susan for a more in-depth chat, but before I could I got another call from Dobbs. It was a foregone conclusion at this point, but he confirmed that the aid was officially cancelled.

There were many people to call, many things to do. But at that moment, at 6:03 on Christmas Eve morning, I decided to treat myself to another cup of coffee and a few moments of peace. I sat down and took in my view of the Golden Gate and the San Francisco Bay. It was still dark outside, but the skies were clear and the last stars were shining.

It was going to be a beautiful, sunny day.

By 7:50 am I had gotten to my union's hall at North Point, where I exchanged greetings and congratulations with Shirley and Dolores. They were setting up for an open house we always ran for our members, both active and retired, during the holiday season. I helped them set up the tables and put up decorations, all three of us ho-ho-hoing to get into the spirit of things. It was the first time this year it had felt like Christmas.

I left the women to place a call to Tom Augustine. I was sure he was being bombarded with calls all morning, but I wanted to get in there to get a chance to say thanks. We had a brief but lovely chat, agreeing on how shockingly fast things had moved. Tom called this day "an incredible victory for the people of El Salvador and all those who opposed militarism and authoritarianism," which I just had to agree with. We left things off by saying we'd get a proper chance to talk over the holidays, once things had died down a little.

Soon Frank Spaulding, Ron Curtice, Gordon Wright, Jimmy Fletcher, and Ki Wu, one of the Local 10 benefits office staff, all showed up to celebrate with and say farewell to Susan. A moment later, the woman herself walked in. She was no longer dressed in the outfits she assembled to tail me in my union work, but a stunning white blouse and pencil skirt. Whatever she wore though, she was a beauty.

"Victory to the union!" she exclaimed, and everyone met her with a cheer.

Smiles, holiday cheer, and good tidings began to whirl around. With Dolores and Shirley leading, we hoisted our cups and glasses to drink "To the health and happiness of our very dear sister Susan."

Susan beamed and sparkled as she said: "Thank you all so very much for helping me see and understand the work of your truly remarkable union!"

Frank turned and asked me to say a few words. I said that I deferred to him as our elder statesman. He chuckled and said: "Elder statesman? I suppose that's a compliment?" Which got a laugh all around.

Everyone's attention was rapt as he ran over the events of the past few weeks. We all got involved, hurling cheers when he mentioned a moment of victory and boos when he got to a nefarious tactic of the bosses or the DOD. The only sober moment was when he invited us to consider the plight the Salvadoran people still faced.

"In short," he concluded, "hopefully our refusal might help to keep El Salvador from becoming another Vietnam."

This was met with a raucous round of applause, and we all took a drink. Right about then it was time for Susan and me to go. Everyone told her that she should come back when our union had to refuse to work another cargo. Meanwhile, Frank told me that when I got back from the airport, he and his ever-loving were hoping to have me over for a bite, a couple of horns of beer, and a full debrief. I said that sounded great, and after many long and bittersweet farewells, Susan and I were on the road.

We stopped off at GHQ to say adios to Paul and his uptown crew with hugs and all the rest. When we arrived at his office, Paul bolted from his chair to give each of us a bear hug. With a big smile and slight bow, he invited her to sit for a few minutes.

"So, here you are, on your way home," Paul said. "You must come back to see us when things are not so rushed or so darned chaotic."

"And when might that be?" Susan asked.

"Now, there's a good question."

"And would you mind another?"

"Oh, not at all. Just fire away."

"Well, I'd like to know, now that I'm departing, what do you think has come down?"

"Now, that *is* a good question." Paul took a moment to consider. "At least to me, what happened here has been a classic response from the union, just like Chile in '78. The stakes were high, the risks great, but we dove into the situation together even knowing it left us no room for retreat. All because of solidarity."

After more hugs and good-byes, we were over to the Archdiocese building. Tom's office was an even larger version of swirling and whirling than it had been at Local 10 or at Franklin Street. I only nodded and smiled briefly as I paid my respects to Father McGinnis, Sister Mary Margaret, and Sister Catherine Anne, speaking a little longer with Tom Augustine and Maria Martinez. Then I retreated to an empty table in the furthest corner of the room while Susan enjoyed a little more of the swirl around her.

We made it to SFO airport in no time at all, the roads being quiet. Once I'd parked and helped her with her bags, we found a booth with seats beside a window in a quiet and nearly empty bar next to her gate. She had a seltzer and lime and I had a vodka on ice. For the first time since the two of us had started spending time together, we were not surrounded by chaos. Although we were sitting quietly and still, it felt like everything was moving too fast.

As I sipped my drink and we laughed and reminisced, I was consumed by a pang. I didn't want her to leave. At least not like this. And yet when it came to putting my feelings into words, I didn't even know where to begin.

After a long and loaded silence, I raised up my glass. All I could muster for words was, "How strange life seems."

Instead of taking a drink, she just shook her head, leaned in, and brushed my cheek with a kiss. In that flash of a moment, I was Bogart and she, Bacall.

"Why'd you do that?

"To see if you'd like it."

"Oh, I liked it for sure. What about you?"

"I knew *I* would."

"Without any help?"

"I'll give you a second chance."

I took her in my arms and gave her a long, sweet kiss. We held each other tight, not wanting the moment to ever end.

When we finally separated, she said, "I'm coming back on the eighth of February."

A rush rippled throughout my body. "You…you're coming back?"

She gave me a look as if to say, "Shame on you for even thinking I'd leave forever."

"For…work?" I said.

"An activist's work is never done. I have a trip to see Brother Chavez and Dolores Huerta. And three days after that, I'm set to see the chair of each one's staff and some of their coworkers."

"Oh. I see. That sounds like a lot of work. You think you might be needing some… help?"

She smiled with a smile that could melt the coldest heart. "Could be. I'm pretty self-sufficient. But if the right person came along…"

Still smiling, she grabbed her purse and stood up. It was time for her flight.

At the gate we agreed that when she got back, we'd have a big talk. They called for boarding her plane and soon after, for her row.

"Have a wonderful holiday," I said.

"You do the same," she murmured. "And think of me."

"Don't worry. I will."

She leaned in, kissed me gently and whispered in my ear: "I'll think of you. Every hour of every day until I'm back here. With you."

And with that, she disappeared through her gate.

For a few moments I just stood there, not knowing where to go or what to do next. The battle was over. We had won. I felt a combination of pride, joy, exhaustion and loss.

As I slowly walked away from the gate, my beeper went off, shaking me out of my reverie. It was Frank. I made my way to the nearest payphone, dropped a dime in the slot and dialed.

"Steve, you're not gonna believe what just happened with Margarito Montebon and Gus Vecenti at their union up the coast. We're gonna want to take action–fast."

Herb Mills

The struggle continues.

Photograph by Joseph Blum

Herb Mills (1930 – 2018) was a long-time leader in Local 10 of the International Longshore & Warehouse Union (ILWU). He earned a PhD in political science from the University of California (Irvine). When asked what he valued most in his life, he would name the ILWU, saying "Thank God for the union," his three children, Sarah, Lydia, and Jon, and the grandchildren. Together with their mothers Rebecca Mills and Deanne Burke, he built a blended family life. He had a great love of nature, and regularly took his children fishing, hiking and camping.

Growing up in Dearborn, Michigan, Herb worked in Ford's legendary River Rouge plant, where he learned about labor unions, and decided to go to college. He was a Phi Beta Kappa graduate from the University of Michigan. He then went into the Army and, after being honorably discharged in California, he went to graduate school, studying political science at University of California, Berkeley. While at Berkeley, Herb taught and became active in the student movement organization called SLATE. In 1960, he served as the picket captain for the Student ACLU picket line at the demonstrations against the House Un-American Activities Committee (HUAC) at San Francisco's City Hall.

In 1963, Herb dropped out of graduate school and became a San Francisco Bay Area longshoreman. On countless occasions, he declared it was "the best decision I ever made!" In 1968 his friend Cleophas Williams, the first Black man elected president of Local 10, granted Herb a year's leave of absence to complete his PhD at the University of California, Irvine. Herb went right back to the waterfront and became active in the ILWU, being elected shop steward, chairman of the stewards' council, business agent and finally, secretary-treasurer of Local 10. He took injury-related retirement in 1991. In January 2018 Local 10 presented him with a lifetime achievement award (https://youtu.be/E12VKEk84Iw?si=jZtP634C3Ufkp1Hc)

Herb was a leader in major conflicts with the longshore workers' employer, the Pacific Maritime Association. He helped lead the 1971-72 strike, the longest in U.S. longshore history. He also led efforts to protect worker health and safety, including a major campaign on the handling of asbestos.

As a union officer, he was the key leader in the ILWU's 1978 refusal to ship military cargo to post-coup d'état Chile, winning support from 175 members of the United States Congress and a final decision by the Carter Administration to cancel the shipment. A similar effort in 1980 stopped military cargo from going to the El Salvador military junta.

When the military government of South Korea announced plans to execute democracy movement leader Kim Dae-jung, Herb took the lead in getting the ILWU to threaten a Pacific Basin refusal by longshoremen to unload South Korean ships. It stopped the execution. Seventeen years later, when Kim was elected South Korea's president, Herb and ILWU President Brian McWilliams were invited to his inauguration as honored guests.

He led efforts to tie the assassination of two young Filipino officials of Seattle ILWU Local 37 to the Ferdinand Marcos' regime.

As a result of this work, their heirs filed a wrongful death suit against Marcos' widow Imelda Marcos and received a $2 million judgment.

In addition to writing the novel *Presente*, he wrote numerous articles and papers about longshore work and the ILWU, acted in two films, and completed an oral history: (https://www.foundsf.org/index.php?title=Oral_History:_Herb_Mills)

Many of his monographs and articles can be found on his web site www.ilwu10hmills.com and in the book edited by Mike Miller *Herb Mills: A Tribute.* Quotations and some of his personal longshore union items are featured in the Transportation exhibit at the Smithsonian National Museum of American History and in the entrance hall to the San Francisco Exploratorium.

Herb Mills collected news articles and correspondence documenting the historic events narrated in Presente, He published these documents on his website - www.ilwu10hmills.com. They cover the union's refusal to load military cargo for El Salvador, its effort to save the life of Kim Dae-jung, Herb Mills' invitation to attend the inauguration of Kim Dae-jung as elected President, and the murder of Filipino union brothers by agents of the Marcos regime. On Herb's website, click on the "ARTICLES" tab and select #12 for more.

AFTERWORD, Peter Cole

The International Longshore & Warehouse Union has a special place in American labor history. It fought fiercely for the rights and benefits of its members. It won a worker-controlled hiring hall that established a fair and equitable system for distributing work rather than one based on patronage, favoritism, or bribery. It was on the front lines of struggles for racial and social justice. It expressed solidarity with workers and other struggles for democratic rights in nations where there were none, and it opposed U.S. foreign policies that supported dictatorships abroad.

The ILWU was born out of the "Big Strike" of 1934, part of a wave of labor militancy across the country. That strike shut down all West Coast ports for six weeks. The 1934 San Francisco General Strike occurred after "Bloody Thursday," the police murder of two striking union members, a longshoreman and a cook, and the injury of 67 others. These strikes were pivotal in the formation of the Congress of Industrial Organizations (CIO) which, in turn, was at the center of the greatest period of mass organizing among working class people in the history of the United States.

Many of the founding generation of leaders and rank-and-filers, nicknamed "'34 Men," were socialists and militant trade unionists who advocated for racial equality. Local 10 was nearly all white at its founding but soon integrated its own ranks. During WWII, the Black membership soared and, by the late 1960s, Local 10 became Black majority. Cleophas Williams, an African American, recalled: "When I first came on the waterfront [in 1944], many black workers felt that Local 10 was a utopia." Williams became the first Black person elected Local 10 President and was re-elected three times.

This ILWU was one of a number of unions expelled from the CIO at the height of the nation's anti-Communist fever after World War II, and the only one that survived fully intact. Thousands of members, including its leader Harry Bridges, suffered ferocious red-baiting. Its strength with its membership made it impervious to efforts to destroy it, whether by political foes or by employers.

In the 1960s, the ILWU negotiated an innovative response to mechanization, but Herb Mills was among the most outspoken critics of these contracts because he believed they undermined the rotating dispatch system at the hiring hall, which he viewed as essential to the union living up to the ideal of equality. So while he admired the International's leadership on many matters, he was also, on those occasions that he thought merited it, a fierce critic. His abiding faith was in the wisdom of an informed rank-and-file. He addressed that rank-and-file vigorously and passionately in his writing and in endless conversations with men on the docks.

In recognition of the women's movement, the International changed its name from "Longshoremen's and Warehousemen's" to the International Longshore & Warehouse Union. While most dockworkers still are men, a growing number of women now work on the waterfront.

Fiercely committed to international working-class solidarity, the union has supported struggles against fascism, military dictatorships, and racism in South Korea, Philippines, El Salvador, Chile, South Africa, and elsewhere. In 1935, Local 10 members refused to load cargo for fascist Italy after it invaded Ethiopia. From 1938 through 1940, they refused to load cargo for imperialist Japan after it invaded China. In 1984, Local 10 boycotted a ship loaded with South African cargo for ten days.

The ILWU has a proud history of commitment to labor and social justice. This book celebrates the best of the union to which Herb dedicated his life.

Herb was always writing. He wrote histories, essays, articles, diatribes, exposés, stories and a few skits, but writing and publishing this fictional memoir, the novel *Presente,* was always his dream, and he worked on it for years. He believed more people would read a novel than nonfiction. He wanted people to feel the passion he and fellow union members felt, to understand the day-to-day business of a union, and see what it took to organize and stand up for justice against powerful opposition. He based the book on his own experiences as a union officer negotiating myriad issues, like job safety and pay equity, while playing a leading role in the historic stand the union took against loading military cargo for El Salvador, and in saving the life of South Korean leader Kim Dae-jung. He died while his last draft was being edited. I promised him we would see it published.

Herb's list of thank you's would begin with the ILWU. "Thank God for the Union!" he often proclaimed. He would thank the men and women who made the ILWU into the democratic, multi-ethnic, powerful, and principled union it became. When in his last years the union awarded him its Lifetime Achievement award, he took the mic and said to the assembled members, "I did it for you."

He would thank Stephanie Fay for her painstaking, rigorous and detailed first round of editing; friend and colleague Peter Cole for believing in the novel, for reading, reviewing, and editing several drafts, Matthew Tallon (Hard Ball Press editor) for his comprehensive and skillful editing, and Tim Sheard, for seeing this as a great story, choosing to publish it, and for his editing and publication.

Herb would thank his family: his children Sarah, Lydia and Jon, and their moms, myself and Deanne Burke, our big extended family, and his many friends, in particular lifelong friends Patricia Lynden and Mike Miller, who read and reviewed his work in progress. I must be leaving out many names he would have included, and I hope you all know who you are.

For more on Herb and his other writing, see Mike Miller's *Herb Mills: A Tribute* and Herb's website www.ilwu10hmills.com.

ACKNOWLEDGMENT, Peter Cole

It's been an honor and privilege to be entrusted with the manuscript that Herb Mills wrote and help turn it into an incredible novel! I first met Herb in 2011 when he invited me to his apartment in South Berkeley. That summer, I was in San Francisco conducting research for my book *Dockworker Power: Race and Activism in Durban and the San Francisco Bay Area*, published in 2018.

While I engaged in archival research across the Bay Area, I also started to interview ILWU members, current and retired. I already knew a few of the deeply impressive Local 10 activists, but connecting with Herb took my excitement to another level. Over the next seven years, I came to respect Herb's tremendous knowledge and intellect, appreciate his important role in advancing one of the strongest, most important unions in the United States, enjoy Herb's company (while drinking countless cups of black coffee from his always- on coffee maker), and even to love Herb.

Dockworker Power benefited immensely from Herb's experiences, wisdom, and insights. I read and re-read many of his brilliant essays about longshore work and the ILWU and continue to consult them. I also formally interviewed, emailed, and spoke with Herb many times.

While working on that book, Herb asked me to edit his unpublished novel. After I completed *Dockworker Power* and while revising my next book *Ben Fletcher: The Life & Times of a Black Wobbly*, COVID-19 rocked our world. Ironically, it was the forced confinement of the first two years of the global pandemic that afforded me the time to fulfill my promise to Herb and help with revisions for his manuscript.

In addition to thanking Herb for writing *Presente*, I can't say enough about the tremendous writing and editing skills of brother Tim! I knew that Hard Ball Press was the right venue for Herb's novel. Fortunately, Tim agreed that *Presente* perfectly fit his publishing mission.

As always, endless thanks and love to my partner, Wendy, who enriches and supports me in countless ways.

ABOUT THE ILLUSTRATOR

Marc Nelson was born and raised in Glen Ellyn, Illinois. Marc earned his Bachelor of Arts degree from Augustana College in Rock Island, Illinois, an Art Education teaching certificate from Western Illinois University, and a Masters in Art degree from Eastern Illinois University. Marc's paintings and drawings have been featured on CNN, BBC, DW, AJ+, NPR, CBC, The New York Times, Amnesty International, award winning documentaries, and other news and human rights agencies and publications. His work has been exhibited nationally and internationally, and appears in public and private collections around the world.. Marc and his wife, writer and educator Jill Bartelt, live and work in Kewanee, Illinois.

Artist website: www.marcnelsonart.com

MORE STORIES FROM HARD BALL PRESS

A Great Vision: A Militant Family's Journey Through the Twentieth Century, Richard March

The Activist Spirt: Toward a Radical Solidarity, Victor Narro

Fight For Your Long Day, Classroom Edition, Alex Kudera

Freedom Soldiers, Katherine Williams

I Still Can't Fly: Confessions of a Lifelong Troublemaker, Kevin John Carroll

Love Dies, Timothy Sheard

The Man Who Fell From the Sky, Bill Fletcher Jr.

The Man Who Changed Colors, Bill Fletchert Jr.

Murder of a Post Office Manager, Paul Felton

New York Hustle: Pool Rooms, School Rooms and Street Corner, Stan Maron

A Pandemic Nurse's Diary, Nurse T with Timothy Sheard

Sixteen Tons, Kevin Corley

Throw Oudt the Water, Kevin Corley

Union Mae, Eric Lotke

With Our Loving Hands: 1199 Nursing Home Workers Tell Their Story, Timothy Sheard, ed.

Winning Richmond: How a Progressive Alliance Won City Hall, Gayle McLaughlin

Woman Missing, A Mill Town Mystery, Linda Nordquist

This Won't Hurt A Bit

Some Cuts Never Heal

A Race Against Death

Slim To None

No Place To Be Sick

A Bitter Pill

Someone Has To Die

One Foot in the Grave

All Bleeding Stops Eventually